THE ROVER BOYS
WINNING A FORTUNE

THE ROVER BOYS
WINNING A FORTUNE

ARTHUR M. WINFIELD

Originally published in 1926.

Published by Wildside Press.
Visit us online at wildsidepress.com.

INTRODUCTION

My Dear Boys:

This book is a complete story in itself but forms the tenth volume in the line issued under the general title, "The Second Rover Boys Series for Young Americans."

In the opening volume of the First Series, "The Rover Boys at School," I introduced my readers to Dick, Tom and Sam Rover and their friends and relatives. That volume and those which followed related the adventures of the three Rover boys at Putnam Hall Military Academy, Brill College, and elsewhere.

Leaving college, the three young men established themselves in business in New York City and became married to their girl sweethearts. Dick Rover became the father of a son and a daughter, as did likewise his brother Sam, while Tom was blessed with a pair of lively twin boys. The four youths were first sent to boarding school, as related in the first volume of the Second Series, entitled "The Rover Boys at Colby Hall," where the lads made a host of friends. During their outings they went with[iv] one of the older Rovers to establish oil wells in Texas and Oklahoma and also went out on Sunset Trail, where we last met them. Their school days had come to an end, and two of the boys were preparing to join their fathers in business when a most disastrous affair occurred. Then the lads went on an ocean trip in an endeavor to aid the family fortunes, and what stirring times their outing led to I leave for the pages which follow to narrate.

Of the twenty-nine volumes issued in this line of "Rover Boys" stories the publishers have already sold *over three and one-half million copies*! To me this is as astonishing as it is pleasing, and I here wish to thank all the young people, as well as the parents, who have stood by me in my efforts to entertain them.

Affectionately and sincerely yours,

Edward Stratemeyer.

CHAPTER I
FRED HAS A SECRET

"SAY, FRED, WHAT IS this secret you're keeping from us?" demanded Jack Rover, as he walked out on the piazza of the old farmhouse where his cousin sat reading a magazine.

"Who said I had a secret?" asked the youngest of the Rover boys, as he laid down the magazine. "I'm sure I didn't say a word about it."

"Nonsense, Fred, you've got something up your sleeve, and you know it!"

"Of course he's got something up his sleeve," put in Andy Rover, who sat on the steps munching an apple. "It's his arm."

"We know well enough, Fred, that you're not roaming around this farm singing 'Down on the Ocean Bottom' day and night for nothing," added Andy's twin brother, Randy.

"What are you talking about—'ocean bottom?' I don't know any such song." But there was a twinkle in Fred Rover's eyes as he spoke.

"We ought to pound the secret out of him—that's what we ought to do," announced Randy. "Come on, you old reprobate, let us in on this, and be quick about it!" and, reaching over, he caught hold of Fred's foot and attempted to drag his cousin from the chair.

"Hi! Let up!" cried Fred, and aimed the magazine at Randy's head. Then he leaped up, broke away from his cousin, and vaulted the piazza railing. An instant later he was dashing across the lawn with the others in pursuit.

As the four boys tore over the grass at Valley Brook Farm three girls came from the house to witness what was going on. They were Mary and Martha Rover and their old school chum, Ruth Stevenson.

"Is it a race?" asked Mary, Fred's sister.

"No; I think they're teasing Fred," said Martha. "They said something about Fred having a secret."

"And he has a secret, too," said Ruth Stevenson.

"What is it, Ruth?" demanded the other girls quickly.

"Oh, I can't tell you that—at least, not yet. Fred told me not to say a word about it."

Across the lawn and down the lane shaded with big trees tore Fred Rover with his three cousins in close pursuit. Then Fred reached the barn, passed through an open doorway, and quickly rolled the door shut behind him.

"Hi, you! Let us in!" cried Jack.

"You keep out of here!" said Fred merrily. "If you don't I'll go for a ride on Carrots."

"Don't you dare touch Carrots!" exclaimed Jack, in alarm. "You leave that horse alone!"

"Maybe he can put some pep in Carrots, Jack, so you'll win the race," suggested Andy.

"Carrots has got pep enough," said the oldest of the Rover boys. "And, anyway, what exercise he needs he's going to get from me."

"Oh, it's too hot to run any more, anyway," came from Randy. "Let's call it off."

"Fred, don't touch that horse, do you hear?" cried Jack.

"Will you promise to leave me alone?" asked his cousin through the closed door.

"Yes. Just the same, I think you ought to let us in on that secret of yours."

"Oh, I'm holding back for your own good," said Fred, and then he allowed the others to pull the door open and they came into the barn.

It was a perfect midsummer day, with a bright blue sky overhead and a gentle breeze blowing from the west. One end of the big barn was already half filled with sweet-scented hay and beyond the building could be seen many acres of growing fields and orchards, all in the best condition.

It was Jack who led the way to where the horse stalls were located. Here, in a box stall, stood a small, wiry, sorrel horse with a white blaze on his forehead. The horse gave a look of recognition as Jack approached and stretched out his head in expectation of some tidbit, and Jack handed him half an apple which he munched contentedly.

"He certainly is a fine-looking animal," was Randy's comment, as the four boys gazed at Carrots. "You certainly ought to win that race, Jack."

"Well, I'm going to try, anyway," was the answer.

"Jack has got to win that race," put in Andy. "If he doesn't he won't dare face Ruth again," and he winked one eye suggestively.

"Oh, say, Andy, you leave Ruth out of this race, will you?" burst out Jack, his face growing red.

"Humph! As if we didn't all know that Joe Sedley is going to race you solely on Ruth's account," went on Andy, who was the tease of the crowd.

"He's going to race me because he thinks his Black Diamond is a better horse than Carrots," returned Jack, "and because he thinks he can ride better than I can!"

"Just the same, Jack, he's got his eyes on Ruth," broke in Randy. "I guess he thinks it would be a grand thing to link the Sedley estate to the new Stevenson estate."

"Oh, you fellows are talking nonsense!" said their cousin, but at the same time Jack's face took on a look of concern.

Valley Brook Farm, where the Rover boys were spending a vacation, was located in the heart of New York State and was the property of their great-uncle, Randolph Rover, after whom Randy had been named. The neighborhood for miles around was exceedingly picturesque and since a new state highway had been put through the land had been in active demand for country residences, by people of means. Below the farm a young man named Joe Sedley, who had inherited a large amount of money from his parents, had purchased an estate of two hundred acres and built himself rather pretentious bachelor's quarters. Directly opposite and adjoining Valley Brook Farm, Mr. Stevenson, the father of Ruth, had purchased another two hundred acres and had now started to put up a large country home.

Because Ruth was so well acquainted with the Rover girls she had often stopped at Valley Brook Farm and her parents had occasionally stayed there overnight while inspecting the work done on the new place next door.

It was on one of her visits to the farm that Ruth one day met Joe Sedley. He had proved himself an agreeable young man and had invited Ruth and the other girls, as well as the boys, to visit his estate and "give it the once over," as he expressed it. Since that time he had been exceedingly attentive to Ruth, much to Jack's discomfiture, for ever since he had known the girl the oldest of the Rover boys had thought Ruth just the finest girl in all the world.

Although Joe Sedley owned both an enclosed car and a sport model, he also possessed several saddle horses, one of them, named Black Diamond, being his especial favorite.

"For a crosscountry racer, I'll wager he can beat anything in this neighborhood," Sedley had once told the Rover boys and the girls.

"Oh, I don't know," Jack had said rather carelessly. "A few months ago Uncle Randolph bought a fine sorrel called Carrots. And believe me, that horse can make some speed!"

"I don't believe he could keep up with Black Diamond—not in a two-mile race, anyway," the young man from across the highway had replied. "Your sorrel may be good enough for a half mile across the country, but after that he'll lag behind."

This talk had led to a spirited conversation in which not only the boys but also the girls took part. Then Randy had suggested a race, and this challenge had been quickly accepted by Sedley and as quickly agreed to by Jack, who usually rode Carrots when he was at the farm and who that morning had been rather nettled by Sedley's constant attention to Ruth. This had been three days before, and the race was to come off on the morrow in the morning, Sedley in the meantime having to go away on business to Rochester.

"Why don't you take Carrots out and exercise him?" said Andy.

"That's what I intend to do," said Jack. "But I won't run him too hard—just enough to make him feel active."

Jack Ness, the old man-of-all-work around the farm, had cleaned the sorrel until Carrots fairly shone from the tip of his nose to the end of his flowing tail.

"He's the best nag in these parts, barring none!" declared Jack Ness emphatically, as he placed the saddle on the sorrel's back. "You sure are going to win that race, Jack."

"I certainly hope to," was the reply. "By the way, has the news leaked out to those living around here?"

"It certainly has, Jack," said the hired man. "Everybody at Dexter's Corners knows about it. Mr. Sedley was down to Woddie's store before he left and also at the railroad station and he told everybody how he was going to put it over you. You'll have quite a crowd to witness the run. Some folks are putting quite some wagers on it," added the old man.

Joe Sedley, having perhaps more money than was good for him, had done his best to draw Jack and his cousins into making a bet for a large amount, but this the boys had declined.

"He could clean us out easily enough," was the way Fred had expressed it, "while the loss of one or two thousand dollars—or even more—wouldn't make him wink."

"Well, I'm not in the betting business," Jack had said briefly. He did not add that he had promised his father not to bet on horse races of any kind.

Early the next morning Joe Sedley telephoned over asking for Ruth and then invited her and the girls to use his sporting car in following the finish of the race, which was to take place on a road ending near the two farms. The invitation rather pleased Ruth, but nevertheless she declined, stating that she had already arranged to go out with Martha and Mary.

"He's got a crust to telephone over to Ruth!" was the way Fred expressed himself when he heard of this. "He knows well enough how matters stand between her and Jack."

"Well, I guess he thinks it's a case of the best man winning," said Randy. "And you've got to admit that he's rather a nice sort, too, although I think his money is spoiling him a little."

Of course Jack was not present at this conversation. But he, too, heard of how Sedley had telephoned, the news being conveyed to him by his sister.

"Jack, you've got to keep your eye on that fellow," declared Martha. "He's doing everything he can to get into Ruth's good graces."

"I know it, Martha, and it makes me mad to think of it! But what can I do to prevent it?"

"You don't think Ruth cares for him, do you, Jack?"

"I don't know. He's got a barrel of money—I know that!"

"You don't suppose Ruth would let that influence her, do you?"

"You ought to know better than I do, Martha."

"Well, I wouldn't if it was me!" said the sister loyally.

It was another perfect day, and when the time for the race came several hundred people were found lining the course which led around several roads in something of a circle, starting at the lower end of the Sedley farm and finishing on a roadway between Valley Brook Farm and the new Stevenson estate.

Both of the horses, as well as their riders, looked in the best of condition as they came forward to begin the race. The course had been carefully mapped out and watchers were stationed along the route to see that no short cuts might be taken by either participant. Even old Uncle Randolph was present and likewise the old colored servitor of the Rovers, Aleck Pop.

"I done got a rabbit's foot fur you, Massah Jack," whispered Aleck just before the race, and brought forth the foot in question, wrapped in a handkerchief. "Dat am suah good luck fur you."

"Thank you, Aleck. I'll be sure to win now," said Jack.

But even though he spoke thus confidently, Jack realized that he had a hard contest before him. Joe Sedley was an experienced rider and Black Diamond a horse that had won more than one crosscountry contest. Jack knew he could take two of the streams which were to be crossed and also several hedges as well as any horse in that neighborhood. Carrots could jump well also, but Jack relied more on his steed's running than anything else.

"All ready?" shouted the starter presently, and then, an instant later, came the report of a pistol and the two contestants were off.

CHAPTER II
THE ROVERS AND SOME OTHERS

"THEY'RE OFF!"

"Ride for all you're worth, Jack!"

"You can win this race without half trying, Sedley!"

"Don't forget Heddon's brook—it's a bad one!"

Such were some of the cries, mingled with cheers, as the two riders dashed away on the two-mile race. Soon they were well on their way down the road, followed for a short distance by a number of people in automobiles and on motorcycles.

"Sedley is ahead!"

"Yes; but Jack Rover is a close second!"

The first quarter mile of the race was over a level road and easy. Then the two contestants turned into a side road and were lost to view among the trees and bushes. Here the automobiles and motorcycles following had come to a halt.

"Wish we could have followed them on horseback," remarked Randy.

"Well, that wasn't to be permitted, so all we can do is to go back to the finishing point and wait for 'em to come," said Fred.

"Oh, Fred, do you think Jack will really win?" asked Ruth.

"I don't see why not. Of course, Joe Sedley has had lots of experience in riding and his Black Diamond is sure a fine runner. But Jack has just got to win, and that's all there is to it!"

The Rover girls and Ruth had brought their cameras with them, and all had taken snapshots of the start of the race. Now they fixed their cameras so that they might get other snapshots of the finish.

"But I won't want any snapshot if Jack comes in second!" declared Martha.

"Oh, well, I want a picture, anyhow," said Ruth. "If Mr. Sedley wins he'll be glad to have a picture of the event."

In the meantime Jack and Sedley were riding for all they were worth, cheered on by friends and neighbors lining the roadway of the race.

Joe Sedley had taken the lead at the start and held it at the end of the first half mile. Then the two contestants turned into another road where the going was unusually rough, and here Jack gradually pulled up until the two horses were neck and neck.

"Here is where I'm going to pass you, Sedley!" cried Jack gayly.

"It's the last lap that counts, Rover!" yelled the rich young man in return.

A little further on they took the first of the two streams to be crossed. Some days before Jack had inspected this carefully and now he reined up Carrots at a point where the steed could get a good footing. Over they went with ease, Black Diamond and his rider immediately following. Then they took to a narrow road running to the rear of Valley Brook Farm.

By the time the first mile had been covered the pace was beginning to tell on both horses. Then came the point where they had to take two hedges in quick succession. Carrots took the first with scarcely an effort, but for some unaccountable reason shied at the second. Black Diamond and his rider shot ahead, and when Jack finally brought his mount over he found himself a good fifty yards to the rear.

"I've got to make it up! I've simply got to do it!" he muttered to himself, and, setting his teeth hard, he urged Carrots forward in a desperate effort to overtake Sedley.

Then came another turn and the riders crossed the state highway and came out on a stretch of road leading behind the Sedley estate. Here going was again rough, but this seemed to please Carrots better than it did Black Diamond and at a mile and a half Jack found himself only a length behind his opponent. Then each rider settled himself for the struggle on the homestretch.

"Here they come!" yelled Andy, as he looked down the roadway.

"Joe Sedley is in the lead! Hurrah!" shouted one of that young man's admirers.

"Oh, don't tell me Jack's going to lose!" murmured Martha.

"Come on, Jack! Come on! You've got to win!" shouted Fred. "Come on!"

As the two riders drew closer there were all sorts of shouts and cries. In the midst of this the girls, and also several other spectators, prepared to take snapshot pictures of the finish.

"Joe Sedley is still ahead! He wins the race!"

"Jack Rover is crawling up!"

"It's neck and neck!"

"Come on! Come on! Let the best man win!"

By this time everybody was wildly excited and it was almost impossible for those in charge to keep the spectators off the road. It was seen that Joe Sedley was riding well, even though Black Diamond showed evidences of the herculean exertions the steed had made. Only a few feet behind came Carrots, his tail flying out and Jack bending well over the sorrel's neck.

"It's Sedley's race!"

"Not much! Rover will pass him!"

"Here they come neck and neck!"

"It's a tie!"

"That's right—it's a tie, sure enough!" came from a score of throats, and then the two riders with their steeds flashed by and the race was over.

"Oh, Fred! was the race a tie?" asked Ruth, as she and the other girls were putting their cameras away.

"I'm afraid it was," said the youngest Rover boy.

"I don't think it was a tie," declared Andy. "It looked to me as if Jack was at least six inches ahead."

"That's the way it looked to me, too," said his twin.

"Rover ahead? Nonsense!" cried one of the Sedley supporters. "If anybody was ahead it was Joe."

"Oh, it was a tie, and that's all there is to it," put in a gentleman who lived at Dexter's Corners. "They'll have to ride it over again."

It was the consensus of opinion among those who had seen the finish of the race that it had been a tie.

"We'll let the photographs decide it," declared Fred. "A whole lot of pictures of the finish were snapped. They ought to tell the tale. Come, what do you say?" he went on to the young man who had been managing the race for Joe Sedley.

"I'm willing to go by the photographs if they're clear enough," was the reply.

"Well, photographs don't lie," said the gentleman from Dexter's Corners.

And now while Jack and Joe Sedley are turning back to the finish line to find out how the race was really decided let me take a few minutes of the readers' time in which to introduce my characters to those who have not met the Rovers before.

In the first volume of this line of books, entitled "The Rover Boys at School," I introduced three wideawake American lads, Dick, Tom and Sam Rover, and told how they left their home at Valley Brook Farm to go to school. From school they went through college, having many adventures in the be-tween-times, and then settled down in business in New York City, forming The Rover Company, with offices in Wall Street.

The three young men married the sweethearts of their school and college days, and as a result of these unions Dick was blessed with a son and a daughter, Jack and Martha, Sam followed with a son and a daughter, named Fred and Mary, while the fun-loving Tom came forward with a lively pair of twins, called Randy and Andy.

At this time the three Rover families lived in three connecting houses on Riverside Drive overlooking the Hudson River. At first the young folks attended the local schools, but soon the boys' propensity for fun and "cutting up" became so pronounced their elders thought it would be better to send them to some strict boarding school.

Colonel Colby, a school chum of the older Rovers, had established a first-class military academy, and in the first volume of our Second Series, entitled "The Rover Boys at Colby Hall," was related how Jack, Fred and the twins went to that institution of learning and made many friends, including Gif Garrison and Spouter Powell, the sons of their father's chums. At the same time Mary and Martha attended a nearby boarding school where they became intimately acquainted with Ruth Stevenson and May Powell, a cousin to Spouter.

A number of years had passed since the younger Rovers had first attended Colby Hall, and during that time they had had a number of thrilling adventures on Snowshoe Island, under canvas, on a hunt, in the oil fields, at Big Horn Ranch and at Big Bear Lake. They had also been shipwrecked, and had been abducted and held for a heavy ransom, as related in the volume preceding this, entitled "The Rover Boys on Sunset Trail."

During the days at the military school and while on their numerous outings the Rover boys had made a great number of friends and also a number of bitter enemies. Some of their enemies had paid the penalty of their misdeeds and were now in prison, but others were still at large and eagerly awaiting an opportunity to do the Rovers an injury.

While at Colby Hall Jack had worked his way up until he became the major of the school battalion, while Fred became captain of Company C. Andy and Randy had been too full of fun to go in for military honors, but had taken their part in numerous sporting contests. When the time came for graduating from the school all of the boys had passed with flying colors, much to their parents' delight.

"The kids are all O. K., even if they're full of fun," said Tom Rover proudly to his wife, Nellie.

"Well, you can't blame them for being full of fun, Tom," returned his wife, with a twinkle in her eye. "You were always chock-full of fun yourself—you know you were," and she poked him affectionately in the ribs.

"Indeed!" said Tom very innocently. "Why, I always thought I was a model young man, as well as a model husband," and then he ducked as Nellie made a move as if to catch him by the hair.

On leaving Colby Hall, the Rover boys had been undecided regarding what to do next. There had been some talk of going to college, but both Jack and

Fred had intimated that they would like to go into business in Wall Street with their fathers. Andy and Randy declared for a trip around the world or "some kind of an outing somewhere."

"I think we might as well let the boys rest and think it over," said Dick Rover to his brothers. "They have been to school steadily for years. It won't hurt them to let them go their own way for a while."

So it had come about that the boys, as well as the girls, were allowed to journey from New York City by automobile to the farm at Dexter's Corners where old Uncle Randolph, Aunt Martha, and Grandfather Rover still resided. Grandfather Rover was now very old and did little but sit in his chair and read the papers.

From his first meeting with Ruth Stevenson some years before, Jack had been greatly attracted by this young lady. She had been a good chum on more than one occasion and he had awakened to his real feelings for her when, through the actions of one of his enemies, Ruth had been in danger of losing her eyesight. This feeling had grown in intensity, and it was this which made Jack feel that he would like to settle down in business so that he might be in a position to ask Ruth to become his wife. He had thought it delightful that the Stevensons had purchased the land adjoining Valley Brook Farm and were about to build a summer residence there. But the entrance of Joe Sedley upon the scene had caused him some misgivings. Sedley was handsome, as well as rich, and owned a beautiful estate directly opposite that purchased by Mr. Stevenson. More than this, the young man had a manner which seemed to please Ruth not a little.

"Well, I suppose he's got as much right to her as I have," Jack told himself several times. But even as this thought coursed through his mind he felt a sudden sinking of the heart, such as he had never experienced before.

CHAPTER III
AN ODD DISAPPEARANCE

"WE HAD BETTER DEVELOP those pictures as soon as possible," said Jack after he had been told that the others had agreed to reserve a decision on the race until the various photographs taken had been examined.

"I'm afraid I didn't get a very good picture," declared Martha. "Just as I got ready to snap it some man jumped up in front of me, waving his hat."

"I was almost in line with the tape, so my picture ought to be a good one," declared Ruth. "I had the diaphragm wide open and the shutter set for the fastest time possible."

"We'll have to be very careful in developing those pictures—we don't want to spoil them," put in Randy.

Joe Sedley was plainly annoyed over the fact that most of the spectators considered the race a tie.

"I think I was a full head to the good," he declared emphatically. "Black Diamond was going as never before and in another fifty yards he'd have been a length ahead."

"Well, we'll have to see what the pictures have to say," said Jack. "Then, if it really was a tie, we'll have to run it over again."

"What do you think it was, Ruth?" asked Sedley.

"I can't say exactly, Joe," the girl said. "You both went past so very fast. But I snapped a picture, and so did the others, and perhaps they'll tell the real story."

"Well, I think it was up to the judges to render a decision and not wait for those photos," said the rich young man. "But of course I'm willing to do what Rover does," and then Sedley rode away to join some of his friends.

The crowd, and especially those who had placed bets on the race, was keenly disappointed and a number of arguments started, some ending in wordy quarrels. The judges of the race asked that all photographs snapped at the finish be submitted to them if possible by the following morning.

So far the day had been ideal, but now a sudden summer shower was coming up and this caused the crowd to scatter rapidly, and the Rovers and Ruth lost no time in getting back to Valley Brook Farm.

Some years before the Rover boys had fitted up a developing and printing room in the old farmhouse, using for that purpose a side pantry which had running water. Randy and Fred were the two who had most interested themselves in the photographic art, and they took the exposed films to learn as quickly as possible what they might show.

"You've got to be careful," cautioned Jack. "If you spoil them Sedley may say you did it on purpose, just to hide the fact that he won."

"Oh, Jack what a mean thing to say of Joe!" cried Ruth.

"Well, I wouldn't put it past him to say it," declared Jack. "He thinks he's the king-pin of everything when he's on Black Diamond," he added somewhat bitterly.

"You wouldn't want Joe to talk that way about you, would you?" went on the girl earnestly.

"Oh, I wouldn't quarrel about it, Ruth," put in Mary before she had given a thought to what her words might lead.

"I'm not quarreling," and then, after a somewhat awkward pause, Ruth turned, picked up a magazine from the center table, and sat down on the piazza to read.

"Mary! How could you?" whispered Martha.

"Why, I—I—didn't mean anything," faltered Fred's sister.

"Yes, but don't you see what Jack—" began Martha, and then suddenly stopped. Then, as Jack and the others moved toward the pantry where the pictures were to be developed, Martha went upstairs and Mary slowly followed.

The day had begun brightly enough, but now it seemed about as dismal in the house as the shower was making it outside. Twice Jack thought of joining Ruth on the piazza, to smooth out the difficulty between them, but for some reason could not bring himself to do it.

"She's got Sedley in her mind," he told himself bitterly. "For all I know, she may hope he won." Yet even as he thought this another thought came that perhaps he was doing Ruth an injustice.

When developed, it was found that Martha's film had been completely ruined by the man who had jumped up in front of her when she snapped it. But those taken by Ruth and Mary, as well as by Fred and Randy, were fairly clear. But all of the pictures were rather small and none of them could be judged clearly in the dim red light of the developing pantry.

"We'll have to dry them and get prints from them before we can be sure of what they show," declared Fred; and then this rather tedious process was begun.

After the race Jack Ness had ridden over to Dexter's Corners to get the mail. Now he came back with a handful of letters which were distributed to the young people.

"Here is something that you fellows will be interested in," declared Fred, as he read a letter from his father. "Dad says old Josiah Crabtree is out of jail again."

"Out of jail again?" cried Jack. "I thought he was let out of jail some years ago!"

"So he was," said Randy. "But I guess you've forgotten that he was put in again on account of some irregularities in connection with selling some stock in a fake university out in St. Louis."

"Do you suppose old Crabtree will try to make trouble for our folks?" went on Fred.

"It's more than likely," said Jack. He and his cousins had learned a great deal concerning this ex-teacher who had done so much harm to the older Rovers in the past.

"Why can't he turn over a new leaf like Dan Baxter and his father did?" was Randy's comment.

"The answer to that is that some people would rather be bad than be good," returned Fred, and then he added quickly: "Do you suppose Crabtree would come after us, the same as Davenport did?"

"There is no telling what a man of that calibre will do," said Jack. "The only thing for us to do is to be on our guard against him."

Then the boys turned again to their letters.

"Here is news!" cried Andy. "Dad tells me that before long he's going to take another trip out to the Rolling Thunder gold mine."

"And my dad says he's going to take another trip down to the oil fields in Oklahoma," came from Jack. "Gee, I'd like to go with him! We'd have a chance to visit Phil Franklin and a lot of other people we know."

"And I'd like to go out to Sunset Trail again!" cried Randy. "We certainly did have good times out there."

"Not while we were kept prisoners in that cave by Davenport and his gang," broke in his brother.

"You fellows hold your horses about going down to Oklahoma or out to Sunset Trail!" cried Fred. "Perhaps there will be something better coming. Who knows?" And then he began to hum softly to himself. "Down on the ocean bottom, boys! Down on the ocean bottom!"

"Say, Fred, for cats' sake, stop that singing and let us know what you've got in your mind!" cried Andy. "You keep on that way, and you'll have us all bughousey."

"Let's pound it out of him, boys!" exclaimed his twin, and caught Fred by the arm.

"No, you don't!" shouted Fred. "I'll tell you about my secret when I'm ready, and not before." And then, as the others tried to catch hold of him, he squirmed away and ran through the dining room and then the sitting room of the old farmhouse.

"My land sakes, boys! what are you up to now?" shrilled old Aunt Martha, who sat by a window shelling peas.

"Fred's got a secret and won't let us in on it!" exclaimed Randy.

"I think he's got a barrel of prunes hid away somewhere and is eating 'em all by himself on the sly," added Andy.

"A barrel of prunes?" exclaimed Aunt Martha, in consternation. Then her eyes began to twinkle. "Andy Rover, quit your foolishness and behave yourself. If you continue to make such a noise, Grandfather Rover will think another war has started."

"Well, we've got to make Fred talk up," said Randy, and then he and his twin, followed by Jack, raced after the youngest Rover boy, who had disappeared through a doorway leading to a side piazza. The next instant Fred had leaped out into the dooryard and, despite the rain that was falling, was streaking it in the direction of the big barn.

"Hi! You'll get soaked!" yelled Jack. "Come back here!"

"Not on your necktie! I'd rather be soaked than be pommeled."

"I'm going after him!" exclaimed Andy.

"So am I!" added his twin, and away they dashed, and then there seemed nothing for Jack to do but to follow.

The sudden shower had caused the water to flow down the lane. Fred and Randy crossed this in safety, but as Andy approached, his foot slipped and down he went headlong, splashing mud in all directions.

"For the love of Pete!" gasped Jack, as several drops of muddy water hit him in the face, one landing in his eye. "What's the idea? If you want to swim why don't you go down to the brook?"

"Wow!" spluttered Andy, scrambling to his feet. His hands and his knees were covered with mud, which was also sprinkled liberally over the front of the suit he wore. "Now I'm going to catch him if I die for it!" he went on, dashing forward.

By this time Fred had reached one of the big sliding doors of the barn and had passed inside, sliding the door shut after him. When the others came up they found the door bolted on the inside.

"Hi! Open that door—and be quick about it!" shouted Randy. "Do you want us to get drowned?" for the rain was now coming down harder than ever.

"I'm not going to open the door!" shouted back Fred. "Go on back to the house!"

"Come on around to the other door," said Jack.

The three Rovers ran around a corner of the barn, but Fred was ahead of them and just before they arrived he shot another bolt into position, so they found this barrier also closed against them.

"Hi, Fred! Have a heart and open up!" demanded Andy. "I need washing, but I don't want to take it out here in the open."

"Come on with me," whispered Randy. "We'll surprise him," and then he hurried the others around another corner of the barn where an opening led to a small pit. From this pit a flight of steps ran up to the main floor of the building. There was a trapdoor here, but this was unfastened and thus the three boys gained entrance to the barn without further trouble.

"Now you'd better surrender!" cried Jack, rushing forward, followed by the twins.

Then, as Fred was nowhere in sight, the three began a search for their cousin. Much to their surprise, he was not to be found. They went through the building from top to bottom half a dozen times, looking into the box stalls and also the harness closet, and peering around the old carriages still stored in the place.

But it was all to no purpose! Fred had totally disappeared!

CHAPTER IV
ALECK SEES A GHOST

"Where do you suppose he went to?"

"Search me! He has certainly dropped out of sight entirely."

"Perhaps he slid out through one of the doors and went back to the house and is now laughing at us," suggested Andy. He was busy wiping the mud from his hands with an old salt bag.

"No, he couldn't have left by any of the doors, for they're all bolted on the inside," declared Jack.

"Maybe he went up in the loft and dropped from one of the windows," suggested Randy.

The three boys took another look around, shouting Fred's name several times as they did so. Then they went up in the loft. Here a grimy window stood half open.

"That window has been opened since we came," declared Andy. "Just the same, he could easily drop out of it to the pile of hay below," he added, looking down.

"We might as well go back to the house and see if he's there," said Jack, and thereupon the three boys descended to the lower floor of the barn, unlocked one of the doors, and made a quick dash for the farmhouse.

"I'm going to wash up a bit before I look for him," said Andy. "I feel as dirty as a sewer digger."

"And you look worse than that," added his twin, with a laugh. "Come on, Jack, let us find Fred and make him tell us his secret," he added to his cousin.

A few minutes after the three boys left the barn Aleck Pop entered the place to get a peach basket which the cook wanted. The colored man had been told that the baskets were in the far end of the barn where Jack Ness had placed them.

"I don't see why Jack couldn't've brung dat basket," mumbled Aleck, as he stumbled along in the semi-darkness of the barn. He considered that all work around that place belonged to the hired man and not to himself, he being employed principally around the house and on outside errands.

The colored man was still some distance from the back end of the barn when he heard a strange thumping. He came to an abrupt halt and began to scratch his woolly pate.

"What's dat knockin'?" he demanded. "Who's dar?"

The thumping ceased and all was quiet around the barn except for an occasional sound from the stalls where several of the horses were munching hay. Then Aleck took another step or two forward.

At once the thumping started up again, coming so loudly and seemingly so near that the colored man gave a suspicious jump.

"Who's dar?" he cried again. "Who's dat knockin'? Is some of you boys playin' a trick on old Aleck?"

Again the thumping ceased, and now it was so quiet in the darkened barn that Aleck seemed to feel his scalp rising. He was naturally superstitious, and at once began to imagine all sorts of things.

"You can't play no tricks on me!" he exclaimed rather weakly. "You come out o' hidin', whoever you is!"

"Goof! Goof! Kerchoo! Goof!" came in muffled tones, and this was followed by a thumping that made poor Aleck turn as if to run. "Goof! Goof!"

Straining his eyes in the semi-darkness of a back corner of the barn, Aleck made out a long and heavy box, the lid to which was tightly closed. Then, as he stood stock still but ready to run away if necessary, he became aware that the strange thumping and other noises were coming from this receptacle.

"Must be a dog or a hog in dat box," he muttered. "But why don't he raise de lid and pop out?"

As the strange sounds and thumping continued, Aleck timidly and fearfully took several steps forward, and then, by peering closer, saw that not only was the lid of the box tightly closed but a hasp used for a padlock had fallen into place over a staple, so that the lid could not be pushed up from the inside.

"Dat dog or hog or whatebber it am, am sure a prisoner," he murmured, and then something like a grin came over his ebony face. Stepping closer, he unclasped the hasp and threw back the long and heavy lid of the box.

"Goof! Goof! Kerchoo! Goof!" came in a splutter from the bottom of the box, and a moment later there arose to the astonished gaze of Aleck Pop a tall figure in white, waving two ghostlike arms wildly.

"Land of Abraham!" shrieked the colored man, and began to tremble from head to foot. "It am a ghost! It sure am!" Then he turned to flee.

"Goof! Goof! Kerchoo!" came from the ghostlike figure. "Kerchoo! Say, somebody—kerchoo—dust me—kerchoo—off—kerchoo—will you? Goof! Goof!" and the figure continued to splutter and make all sorts of mysterious movements.

"It's a ghost! It's a hant!" shrieked Aleck, and rushed out of the barn and toward the house as fast as his aged legs would carry him. He burst into the kitchen, rolling his eyes wildly.

"Aleck! Aleck! What is the matter with you?" cried Aunt Martha, in consternation.

"Der am a ghost in de barn, Mrs. Rober!" was the scared reply. "A great big white ghost!"

"Oh, Aleck, there are no such things as ghosts," was the ready reply of the old lady. "You are surely mistaken."

"But I done saw it! It rose out of a box and waved long white arms at me!"

"What's that about a ghost, Aleck?" asked Jack, as he came in, followed by the twins.

"I done saw a ghost in de barn. Came out of a big box down in a back corner. It was all white and groanin' and moanin' something terrible. I think somebody's gwine to die!" and Aleck rolled his eyes in fright.

"It must be Fred," declared Randy. "Aleck, it's Fred, and he's playing a trick on you."

"How could dat be Fred? Who locked him in dat box?"

"Was he locked in?" asked Randy quickly.

"He sure was. De hasp of de lid was slipped over de staple."

"Then there's the answer to the riddle," announced Andy. "Fred got in the box and couldn't get out again."

"But dat ghost am all white—jest as white as a ghost could be," declared Aleck emphatically.

"If he was locked in the box, why didn't he make some kind of a noise when we called him?" asked Jack.

"Let's go and make sure!" cried Randy.

Regardless of the rain, the three boys hastened once again to the barn and rather sheepishly Aleck Pop followed them. A ludicrous sight met their gaze as they entered. Standing in the middle of the barn floor was Fred trying with a handkerchief to get a whitish substance from his face, and especially from his eyes and nose. He was spluttering and sneezing and coughing all at the same time.

"Goof! Goof! Kerchoo! I'm almost—kerchoo—dead with this—this stuff!" he spluttered. "Here, lend me a handkerchief or—kerchoo—something. I—I can't get my breath!" and he continued to splutter for several minutes.

In the meantime Jack thumped him on the back and the others did what they could think of to relieve him. His clothing was covered with a fine, light, flour-like substance, and this had gotten into his ears and hair, as well as into his eyes and nose.

"I know what that is," declared Randy. "It's the new stuff Uncle Randolph bought for spraying in the garden. It takes the place of arsenic and things like that. It's sprayed on dry, and then the rain does the rest."

"My gracious, Randy, do you suppose it's poisonous?" asked Jack quickly.

"If dat stuff am poison, Fred am a dead boy," prophesied Aleck solemnly. Now that he saw that what he had supposed was a ghost was really Fred he felt more like himself.

"I'm going to hunt up Uncle Randolph and find out about this," said Randy, and ran off without further ado. A little later he came back to find the others dusting Fred off with a whiskbroom and a cloth.

"Uncle Randolph says he doesn't think the stuff will do any harm," Randy announced. "But he thinks Fred had better take a bath and change his clothing and be careful not to swallow any of the powder and not to breathe any of it up into his nose."

"You bet I'll take a bath, and do it right away!" was Fred's answer, as he continued to cough and sneeze.

"But how in the world did you come to jump into the box? Didn't you see the stuff in there?" asked Jack.

"It wasn't there when I jumped in—at least, it wasn't there to bother me," said Fred. "It was in a couple of big paper bags. I was all right when you tramped around the barn calling for me, and so I kept quiet. But after you left I tried to get out of the box and found I couldn't. Then I began to thump around, and first thing I knew I kicked the bags apart and then the powder flew all over, and I was almost smothered. Then I began to splutter and kick for all I was worth, and then Aleck opened the box."

"Well, it's a good thing Aleck came," declared Randy. "If he hadn't come, you might have been smothered to death."

"I guess that's right. Aleck, I owe you a good deal for this."

"Dat's all right, Massah Fred," said the old colored man. "Jest de same, jest don't you scare dis darkey to death de next time you get in a box."

"The next time I get in a box I'll keep out of it," declared the youngest Rover, and then hurried to the house to get his bath.

When the girls heard of the mishap that had befallen Fred they were much concerned, even Ruth taking a great interest.

"Oh, Fred, you must be more careful!" cried his sister. "Why, you might have smothered to death!"

"It's just like the old story," said Ruth. "Don't you remember, where the bride hid from her husband and got locked in a trunk in a garret and her skeleton was not found till years and years afterwards?"

"Oh, Ruth, what a horrible story to tell!" burst out Martha.

This happening seemed to bring the young folks together again, and for the time being the little coldness between Jack and Ruth was forgotten. After supper the young folks gathered around the piano for a while and played and sang, and then listened in on a radio which the boys had brought from the city.

"There is something wrong with this radio set," declared Jack, after they had made a number of attempts to get distant stations. "I think the best thing we can do is to look over the aërial to-morrow and see if we've got it just right."

"I think that big elm tree interferes with it," declared Randy.

A little later the boys prepared to make some prints from the films taken of the horse race, using a battery light for that purpose. It had now grown darker and Aunt Martha was going around lighting up.

The boys were still at work over the films, and the girls were in the sitting room with Ruth at the piano, when suddenly Martha let out a scream, and this was followed by a scream from Mary.

"What is it? What's the trouble?" asked Jack, as he came rushing in, followed by the others.

"Somebody looked in at the window!" declared Ruth.

"It was Slugger Brown!" gasped Martha.

"And he made the most awful face at us you ever saw!" added Mary.

CHAPTER V
A GLIMPSE OF ENEMIES

"Slugger Brown!"

"What does that rascal want around here?"

"Where did he go to?"

"Come on and see if he's still outside!"

Such were some of the remarks made by the Rover boys after Martha and Mary had announced that they had seen Slugger Brown peering in at the parlor window of the old farmhouse.

My old readers will remember Slugger Brown well. He had attended Colby Hall while the Rovers were cadets there, and he and his crony, Nappy Martell, had done many things to make life unpleasant for our friends. Then, when Slugger and Nappy were exposed and had departed, these two unworthies, along with their fathers, had continued to cross the Rover boys' path. During the World War Mr. Brown and Mr. Martell had been put in prison as German sympathizers and Slugger and Nappy had been placed in a detention camp in the South. Later on the Browns and the Martells had gone down into Texas and Oklahoma and there aided Carson Davenport and his gang in an endeavor to take away oil claims belonging to Dick Rover. These rascals, as well as another evildoer named Werner, overreached themselves, and as a result sunk all their money in wells which produced but little oil, and in the end the rascals left the fields practically penniless.

"It's queer Slugger Brown should come up here," was Jack's comment, as the boys searched around the house in the semi-darkness. It had stopped raining but the grass and bushes were still wet.

"I often wondered what became of him," returned Randy. "With his money gone, I supposed he had had to go to work."

"I'll wager he and his father and the Martells, as well as the Werners, are as bitter as can be," was Fred's comment. "They would do almost anything to down us for the way things panned out in the oil fields."

"Well, we weren't responsible for their wells running dry," asserted Andy. "They spent their money in their own way."

"Yes, but they'll always lay their failure at our door," said Jack. "All of those chaps think their downfall due entirely to us."

Most of this conversation took place after the boys had run around the farmhouse several times and looked behind various trees and bushes. Not a sign of a lurker could be found.

"Wait until I get a searchlight," suggested Randy, and ran into the house for that article. When he reappeared the light was flashed on the sill of the window where the face of the intruder had appeared and also on the soft ground below.

"There are fingerprints on the wet sill!" cried Jack. "They must have been made since the rain stopped—otherwise they wouldn't be so distinct."

"And here are fresh footprints, too!" added Randy. "Some one was here, that's sure."

"If we were only fingerprint experts perhaps we could tell from them who the fellow was," declared Fred.

"What's the use of that? Martha and Mary both say it was Slugger Brown; and they certainly ought to know, they met Slugger often enough."

The boys visited the barn and other outbuildings, then they flashed the light to a distance. They thought they saw a figure hurrying across one of the fields, but it was very indistinct and they concluded a further investigation would be useless.

The girls had gathered on the piazza and asked numerous questions when the boys returned. Ruth was as concerned as the Rovers, for in the past she had had several unpleasant experiences with Slugger Brown.

"With such a rascal around there is no telling what may happen," said Martha anxiously. "Why, he might even set the house on fire—or something like that!"

"Oh, don't get so scared, Martha!" burst out her brother. "We'll take care of Slugger Brown, if he shows himself again."

"Maybe you girls were mistaken. It might have been nobody but some farmhand or a tramp who looked a little like Slugger," suggested Fred.

"No, it was Slugger, I'm sure of it!" declared Martha, and on this point Mary firmly agreed.

The young folks discussed the subject a few minutes longer, and then, as there seemed nothing further to do concerning the mysterious appearance and disappearance of their enemy, the boys went back to the printing of the photographic films.

The picture taken by Martha was worthless and those taken by Mary and the boys little better. But when Ruth's picture was printed it came out with especial clearness.

"Hurrah! Here we are!" exclaimed Andy, after a close inspection. "This shows Jack nearly a foot ahead!"

"That's right!" said Fred. "Jack won the race, after all!"

"Good for you, Jack! I knew you could do it!" exclaimed Randy, patting his cousin on the shoulder.

"Well, we'll have to see what the other photographs show before we crow too much," announced the oldest Rover boy cautiously. "You know a photograph depends entirely on the angle from which it was taken. Some of the other pictures may show up differently."

Of course the girls were equally interested, and Ruth was proud to think that she had been able to snap such a rapid scene so well.

"It's a good advertisement for this make of camera," the girl declared. "I really ought to send a copy of the picture to the manufacturers. Maybe they might give me a prize for it."

"Why don't you do it, Ruth?" cried Mary. "They often pay good prices for pictures like that, and then reproduce them in the magazine advertising." And thereupon the girls became quite interested in this new subject and Ruth finally agreed to take an extra copy of the picture and send it to the maker of the camera with a letter stating how the photograph had been taken.

This was all perhaps as it should have been, and no one noticed anything unusual but Jack. He could not help but note that Ruth had not said one word to him about winning the race. Had she rather hoped that Joe Sedley would come out ahead?

In the morning two copies of the photograph Ruth had taken were dispatched to the judges of the race, and then the Rover boys prepared to fix the radio aërial. But while they were getting out a ladder and some tools the telephone rang and Jack was called by his Uncle Randolph to answer it.

"Hurrah! What do you know about this?" cried Jack, after the call had come to an end. "Who do you suppose are coming this way? They'll get here in time for dinner!"

"Some of the folks from New York?" asked Mary quickly.

"No. Gif and Spouter! They're on a little tour, and they told me to tell you girls that they have a surprise for you."

"A surprise! What can that be?" asked Martha.

"They didn't say—only said that it was a complete surprise," said Jack.

"Which way are they coming?" asked Fred.

"They're driving this way from Albany in the Powell's sedan. They said they would strike the new highway at Margot."

"Say, what's the matter with going out to meet them?" cried Randy. "This aërial can wait. Perhaps they'll be glad to help us adjust it. Gif knows more about radio than any of us—he's a regular bug on it."

"Oh, I'd like an auto ride this morning! Let's go!" exclaimed Martha. "The air is just lovely after yesterday's rain."

"And maybe by the time we're coming back we can hear how they decided about the race," said Fred.

The Rover boys had not seen their old military academy chums for a long time, and it was quickly agreed that they should take two of the autos and all of the young people should go.

During the other times they had been out in the cars Ruth had always sat on the front seat beside Jack, who usually drove. Now, however, when they were getting ready to go there was an awkward pause. Martha expected Jack to say something to Ruth, but he did not and Ruth held back while the others got in.

"Hurry up, Ruth! Get into your place!" cried Mary. "We ought to be off and see what sort of a surprise Gif and Spouter have for us."

"Oh, I was thinking perhaps some one else would like to sit in front for a change," declared Ruth.

"You're welcome to sit here if you want to," said Jack, but somehow the words did not sound very urgent. Jack still remembered that Ruth had not congratulated him on winning the race.

"Well, Jack, if you don't want me—" murmured the girl in a low tone.

"What?" he stammered, and then, of a sudden, he caught her arm. "Get in, and hurry up. The first thing you know Gif and Spouter will be here and we'll have no ride at all," and the next moment Ruth was in her usual seat and Jack had run around the car and taken his place at the wheel. The other auto was already off, and the second auto speedily followed.

As Martha had said, it was a glorious day after the shower and soon all of the young people were in good spirits as the two automobiles rushed along over the smooth surface of the new highway. In a twinkling they had passed through Dexter's Corners and beyond the railroad station and then began to climb the first of the long hills leading eastward.

"What do you suppose that surprise they have can be?" asked Ruth, as they sped along.

"I've got my own idea," said Jack, in a little bit more friendly tone than he had used before. "But I don't think I ought to tell you, Ruth."

"Why not?" she pouted.

"It wouldn't be fair to Gif and Spouter. But I'll say this—I think it will interest Fred almost as much as it will you girls."

"Oh!" And then Ruth grew suddenly thoughtful. Then she presently glanced slyly at Jack and smiled, and, glancing back, he grinned in return; and thus the thin ice that had been forming between them dissolved.

Mile after mile was covered, and in less than an hour they reached Margot and there brought the cars to a halt.

"It won't be safe to go any further," explained Randy, who was driving the other car. "There are two roads from Albany coming in here, and we don't know which one they are taking. They didn't know themselves, because when they got to Jackville they were going to ask which one was in the better condition and then take that."

While waiting at Margot they entered a drug store and had some ice-cream soda. They had just finished this treat when Fred, who had gone out to see if their friends were yet in sight, came back hurriedly and motioned to the other boys.

"Come out here, quick!" cried the youngest Rover. "I've got a surprise for you! Hurry!"

Grabbing up the change the druggist was giving him, Jack dashed out of the place, followed by the twins. Fred was on the sidewalk pointing in the direction of a side road leading southward from the town.

"See that auto?" exclaimed the youngest Rover excitedly.

"Yes. What of it?" asked Jack.

"It just came up the roadway we have been traveling," said Fred. "There were two people in it. The minute the driver saw me standing by the machines he put on all speed, went around that corner, and now he's streaking it for all he's worth."

"Well, what of that?" asked Randy. "Who was the driver?"

"The driver of that car was Slugger Brown," said Fred. "And do you know who the fellow with him was?" he went on earnestly. "It was Nappy Martell!"

CHAPTER VI
HOW THE RACE WAS DECIDED

"Let's go after them and see what they're up to!"

The words came simultaneously from the twins. As for Jack, he was already running for the car he had been driving.

"Tell the girls!" he shouted back. "Tell them to wait here and keep an eye open for Gif and Spouter."

The girls had already come to the doorway of the drug store, wondering what the excitement was about. Mary held her soda glass in her hand, for she had not yet finished the treat. In a few gasped-out words Andy explained the situation. In the meantime Randy and Fred had piled into the auto and Andy had all he could do to leap upon the footboard as it started up.

"Don't be gone too long!" shouted Martha after them.

"We'll leave word here at the drug store if we go home!" added Mary.

The auto containing the Rover boys rounded the corner on two wheels, and then Jack put on as much speed as he dared while leaving the town. Far ahead on the road leading southward they could see another auto streaking along, leaving a trail of smoke and dust behind.

"We've got to catch them before they reach Barret's Crossroads," declared Jack. "If we don't we won't know which way they went."

The crossroads to which he referred was about a mile and a half distant. Here the road branched in three directions, one heading south and another slightly to the east and the third slightly to the west. The middle highway ran uphill and the two other roads through a stretch of dense woods.

For the first half of the distance the oldest Rover made good time, the speedometer registering between forty and forty-five miles per hour. But then, as they approached a small side road, a load of hay came into view and a few seconds later blocked the highway entirely.

"Hurry up there, you!" shouted Jack, and his cousins repeated this cry. But the old farmer who was driving the load was either deaf or did not care for what they said. He paid not the slightest attention, and seemed to enjoy taking his time in getting around the corner. And even then he blocked the highway so completely that Jack had to drive around and partly into a ditch where for a few seconds the automobile was in danger of overturning.

"Gee, he's a peach for politeness!" was the way Fred expressed himself.

"The auto ahead is out of sight!" groaned Randy. "Step on it, Jack!"

His cousin did "step on it" with the result that for a few minutes the speedometer registered between forty-five and fifty miles per hour, which was a terrific speed, especially when the unevenness of the highway was taken into consideration. Once or twice they struck small hollows and stones and bounced up and down in a most alarming fashion.

"Watch yourself, Jack! We don't want to be turning somersaults," cautioned Andy.

"I've got her under control—don't worry," was the quick reply.

But regardless of the rapid progress made, the delay caused by the load of hay proved disastrous, for the automobile ahead could not be overtaken, and when Barret's Crossroads was reached not a vehicle or a human being of any kind was in sight. In a field near by a dozen or more cows were chewing their cuds, and that was all.

"And the cows can't tell us which way that auto went!" said Andy, in disgust. "Hang the luck, anyhow! If we had only collared Slugger and Nappy we might have found out what they're doing in this neighborhood."

"Yes, and we might make Slugger explain what he meant by looking into the window," added Fred.

The four boys inspected the wagon and automobile tracks in the three roadways, but these were so hopelessly mingled they proved nothing. Then Jack turned the auto around, and they made a quick run back to Margot, where they found the girls in waiting near the drug store corner.

The boys had just explained how they had failed to catch their enemies when they heard the tooting of a horn and the next instant a fine sedan with all the windows down flashed up to them and came to a standstill. Spouter Powell was at the wheel and Gif Garrison sat beside him.

"Hello, everybody!" shouted Gif good-naturedly. "Came to meet us, did you?"

"Glad to see you've got a new highway from here on," remarked Spouter. "The section we just came over is something fearful. I thought I'd break all the springs. How is everybody?" and he leaped out, followed by Gif, and began shaking hands with the girls and boys.

"Oh, what's that surprise you've got for us?" asked Mary eagerly. "We're all dying to know!"

"Well, don't die here, Mary," said Gif, with a grin. "It would be awfully inconvenient to have to carry your body away back to the farm."

"Now, Gif Garrison, don't you start to tease!" said Mary, growing red in the face. "You know well enough what I mean. You and Spouter have a secret. What is it?"

"A real, genuine, dyed-in-the-wool surprise," said Spouter. "The first one to guess it gets a big red apple."

"What have you got under that robe in the back?" asked Ruth, with a twinkle in her eye.

"A barrel of flour and two sacks of potatoes," said Gif glibly.

"Behold the surprise!" went on Spouter, and pulled aside the summer robe just mentioned. From underneath there emerged a close-fitting hat hiding a face just then filled with giggles, and then a small but exceedingly good-looking girl arose to her feet.

"May Powell!"

"Where in the world did you come from?"

"Oh, Spouter, it was just lovely to bring your cousin!"

"I wrote to her two weeks ago to come, but she thought she couldn't," said Martha. "This is certainly the dearest ever!"

Thus speaking, the other girls fairly dragged Spouter's pretty cousin from the tonneau of the car and smothered her with kisses. Then the boys all came in for a hearty handshake, especially Fred.

"Gee, this sure is a welcome surprise!" said the youngest of the Rover boys, and held May's hand so long it made her blush.

"Remember what I said about Fred?" whispered Jack to Ruth on the side. "I thought he'd be as much interested as you girls."

"He certainly seems to be very well satisfied," said Ruth demurely.

And Fred was satisfied, because ever since he had gone to Colby Hall he and May had been the best of chums.

Jack invited the new arrivals to have some soda and while this was being disposed of told his former school chums of the sudden appearance and disappearance of Slugger Brown and Nappy Martell.

"Bad eggs—both of them!" was Gif's comment. "If they're in this neighborhood, you fellows had better keep your eyes open."

"Gif and I have some news for you," remarked Spouter, when finishing his soda. "We'll tell you about it later on. It's just a little business matter."

"Are you fellows going into partnership?" asked Jack quickly.

"No. It's something else," said Gif. "Something I think will please you fellows a whole lot."

On the way home Gif got in the car Fred had occupied while Fred and Mary joined May and Spouter. On the way towards Dexter's Corners the Rover boys told about the horse race and how they were going to stop to see how the judges decided.

"Well, if that photo shows that Jack was ahead they ought to decide the race in his favor," said Gif.

"We haven't seen any of the other pictures yet," said Randy. "They may tell a different story."

"Well, it certainly must have been a close race. I wish I'd been here to see it."

"If they declare it a tie you'll have a chance to see it ridden again."

The judges were to meet at a certain law office at the Corners, and when the Rovers and their friends drove up they found a crowd collected with a number of automobiles and carriages parked along the curb.

"There is Joe Sedley's car," remarked Andy, in a low tone, and pointed to a very fine automobile a short distance away.

"You boys go up into the office," said Martha. "There seems to be such a crowd we won't go. But let us know the news just as soon as you get it!" And so it was arranged.

When the Rovers, followed by their chums, entered the corridor leading to the law office they heard several arguments in tones far from soft and reassuring. Soon they recognized Joe Sedley's voice.

"That's nothing but rank nonsense!" Sedley was saying. "Rank nonsense, and I don't agree to it! If anything, that race was a tie and ought to be ridden over again!"

"We judges don't see it that way," was the answer of one of the gentlemen present, a lawyer named Rockwell. "Here are four pictures, all taken by different persons, and each of these pictures shows that Rover was at least a foot ahead of you at the finishing tape."

"Oh, you can't go by what a photograph shows," growled Sedley. "Cameras play all sorts of funny tricks. It was a neck-and-neck race, and that is all there is to it. If Rover is willing to ride it over again, well and good. But if not, please remember that I claim it was a tie and so far as I am concerned all bets are off. That is all there is to it."

"Wait a minute!" cried Jack, pushing his way forward and confronting the head of the judges' committee. "What is your decision, Mr. Rockwell?" he asked.

"Four photographs show that you were at least a foot ahead at the finish," declared the head judge of the contest. "That being so, we have declared the race in your favor. You win, Mr. Rover, and I congratulate you," and the lawyer shook hands.

"And we congratulate you also," put in the other two judges.

"Humbug!" stormed Joe Sedley. "Humbug, I say! I protest!"

"Your protest will avail you nothing," said Mr. Rockwell sharply.

"We'll see about that! I don't believe anybody around here is going to take my rights away from me!" shouted Sedley, losing his mental balance completely. Then, with a dark look at the Rovers, he strode out of the lawyer's office and stamped out of the building.

"My, but isn't he real sweet!" snickered Andy, in a low tone.

Various comments were made over the abrupt departure of the rich young man. A few of the spectators sided with him, but the majority agreed that he was thoroughly unreasonable. While there was a running fire of comment the Rovers were allowed to look at the pictures which had been used in deciding the race and could see that Jack had won beyond the shadow of a doubt.

"We'll keep these pictures for the present," said Mr. Rockwell. "They'll be returned to their respective owners later."

When the Rovers and the others rejoined the girls they found the latter eagerly discussing the sudden and unceremonious departure of Joe Sedley.

"Why, he never even noticed us!" declared Martha. "He looked as dark as a thundercloud and as mad as a hornet. He dashed over to his car, leaped in, slammed the door after him, and made off as if the very old Nick was in pursuit."

"Well, I don't blame him for feeling bad," said Jack. "But I don't think I'd show it like that if I had been in his place."

"Then, you really won, Jack?" cried May. "Wasn't that grand!"

"If he really thinks it's a tie, Jack, why don't you ride the race over again?" said Ruth. "Perhaps you could give him a worse beating."

"I don't think Jack ought to ride it over again!" declared Martha. "If he won it, he won it, and that's all there is to it."

"That's just what I say!" broke in Mary.

"Well, I think I'd ride it over again rather than have all this fuss and feather and make an enemy of Joe Sedley," declared Ruth, and once again Jack felt that she was raising a barrier between them.

CHAPTER VII
ABOUT SOME INVESTMENTS

"Spouter, you said yesterday you had news for us," remarked Jack on the following morning while he and the twins were showing their chums the radio aërial which had to be fixed. Fred was not present, having gone on a walk with May. The other girls were upstairs discussing the question of what to wear on such an unusually warm day.

"I think it will be news that will please you," returned Spouter. "Anyway, it pleases me and Gif."

"Oh, I know they'll like it! They spoke about it once before," put in Gif. "It's in regard to our dads' investments."

"Oh, are they going into The Rover Company with our folks?" broke in Randy eagerly.

"That's it," said Spouter. "My father has already invested thirty thousand dollars and is going to invest another twenty thousand very soon."

"And my father has put up his full fifty thousand already. Did it two days ago," announced Gif a bit proudly. "So you see we have quite an interest in The Rover Company," and he strutted around with his head in the air and his thumbs in his armholes.

"Will that mean that you'll go into the business with Fred and me later on?" asked Jack eagerly, looking at both of his chums as he spoke.

"I've been thinking of something of that sort," said Gif slowly. "But I'm thinking also of taking up civil engineering."

"I don't think I want to go into Wall Street," said Spouter. "I'm not going to make up my mind this year, but I'm inclined to think I'll take up law. I'd like to go into a court room and address a judge and jury on an important case."

"You could do it all right enough, Spouter," said Randy. "So far as I know, you were never at a loss for words when talking."

"You could talk a jury right into doing whatever you wanted," added Andy merrily. "All you'd have to do would be to keep on spouting until they wanted their dinner or their supper, or wanted to retire for the night, and then you'd have 'em promising you anything, if only you'd let up."

"Humph!" snorted Spouter. "A fine opinion you have of my oratorical ability! Of course I might use an extended argument, but it would be in strict accordance with the facts of the case. I'd lay down a plain proposition, then go into the various and clinching particulars, and after that—"

"Please, Spouter, don't start so early in the morning," pleaded Randy, for he as well as the others knew that if their chum ever got going he would not stop talking for a long while. He had not been nicknamed "Spouter" for nothing.

As had been said, Gif was something of an expert when it came to radio, and soon he located the trouble, both in the radio itself and in the way the aërial had been put up. He and Jack, by the aid of a long ladder manipulated by all of the crowd, managed to get the aërial properly fastened and then the radio was tried out on a distant station and found to work to perfection.

Presently Fred and May came back and the other girls came downstairs, and then the whole crowd took a walk over to the new Stevenson estate. Here the foundations had been put down for the new building and the carpenters were ready to erect the first of the big timbers.

"But dad wrote that the carpenters have another job to finish first," said Ruth; "so they won't do any more here for several weeks. Then they're going at it and keep going until it's finished."

Ruth had studied the blue prints thoroughly, and it was not without considerable pride that she explained how the house was to look when finished and where the various rooms were to be located.

"My room will be right over here on this end, and will have a nice sleeping porch attached," she said. "Won't it be a lovely view? I'll be able to see for miles and miles."

"And you'll be able to swallow ozone by the bushel and the ton," added Andy, with a grin.

After inspecting the spot where the building was to stand the young folks broke up into little groups, and presently Jack found himself walking by the side of Ruth and in the direction of a little brook that wound in and out among the trees. This was near a point where the Rover estate and the Stevenson estate joined.

"Did Spouter and Gif tell you the news about their folks?" asked Jack, as they strolled along.

"What news, Jack?"

"I mean about their dads investing in The Rover Company. Gif's dad has put up fifty thousand dollars and Spouter's dad has put up thirty thousand and is going to put up the other twenty very shortly."

"Yes, I heard about that, Jack," and then Ruth began to color a little. "I suppose you heard about what my father is going to do?" she continued after a moment's pause.

"Your father? No, I didn't hear about that."

"He's going to take fifty thousand dollars' worth of stock, too. In fact, I think he has already done so," and Ruth cast down her eyes while she blushed more than ever.

"Ruth! You don't mean it!" Involuntarily Jack caught her by the arm. "And you never told me!"

"I—I thought—dad ought to speak about it first," faltered the girl. "You know, I didn't want you to think that—" and then she stopped abruptly.

"Why, Ruth, it's wonderful! Just wonderful!" cried Jack, his face glowing. "It shows what faith your dad has in our concern. I guess he knows I'm going in with my father and Fred is going in too, doesn't he?"

"He said that your father had written that you were going into the business later on."

"Why, your dad and my folks and myself will be sort of partners later on, Ruth! Won't that be great?"

"My dad thinks you are all going to make a lot of money," went on the girl.

"We'll sure hope to," said Jack. He was trying to catch her eyes, but Ruth was now looking down into the stream.

"Do you think you'll like to be in Wall Street, Jack?"

"I don't know why not."

"Didn't you used to think something of going into law or becoming a doctor—or something like that?"

"Oh, I used to think all sorts of things, Ruth, just like any other fellow. But somehow neither doctoring nor the law appeals to me. The folks have a real good business in Wall Street, and I think I might as well go in with them as not. Of course I sha'n't spend all my time down there grubbing for money. I'm going to take an interest in our gold mine in the West, and our oil fields in the South, and I think between all of them I'll have plenty to do."

"If you travel South and travel West all the time you'll not be at home very much," was the girl's comment. "I guess you don't care much for society, Jack?"

"Not a great deal. I always thought it was rather a hardship to get into a dress suit, especially in hot weather," and Jack smiled a little.

"Did you get an invitation to the dance over at the Blue Mountain Golf Club next Saturday?"

"No. None of us belongs over there, you know. How did you hear about it?"

"Why, Joe Sedley spoke about it. He said nearly all the best people around here went there."

"Well, there are some nice people go there, but others are not so nice—in fact, the club is getting the reputation for being a little bit swift."

"Mr. Sedley said it was the finest club anywhere around here. He said it was a great honor to belong to it."

"Did he ask you to go to the dance with him, Ruth?" asked Jack bluntly.

"Yes."

There was a moment of awkward silence. It was on the tip of Jack's tongue to say a number of things, but he did not utter a word.

"But I'm not going to the dance," went on Ruth. "I don't want to leave the other girls. And, anyway, the girls are all getting ready, as you know, to visit my home. But I think it was very nice of Joe Sedley to ask me to go," she added.

How far this conversation might have extended there is no telling, because at that moment several of the others came up with the announcement that it was time to return to Valley Brook Farm for lunch, and after the repast Ruth went off with the other girls to complete the arrangements for going home and taking her former school chums with her.

But the conversation made Jack more thoughtful than ever. He wondered if Ruth had not been drawing him out on purpose and wondered also if she would have been better pleased had he announced his intention of taking up some profession.

"Maybe now that her family is well fixed she would like to shine socially," he told himself. "Well, lots of people like that, so I couldn't blame her. But I'm afraid I'd make a poor showing trailing the élite four hundred. And then, what did she mean about traveling out West and down South? Maybe she would prefer somebody who stuck at home. But I couldn't do that—not all the time. It's not in my nature."

But Jack was not left to meditate long. Gif and Spouter claimed his attention and reminded both him and the other boys that they had been promised an outing in the woods back of the farm if they came there for a vacation.

"Both of us are a bit tired of running the car," explained Spouter. "We'd like to get into the wide-open spaces, as they call it, and rough it a bit as we used to on Snowshoe Island and on our big hunt."

"We'll start out on a little trip just as soon as the girls leave," said Randy.

"Provided Fred can break away from May," put in his twin slyly.

"May has certainly got him hypnotized," laughed Jack.

"Humph! What about Ruth having you under her thumb?" retorted the youngest Rover, and then he added quickly: "But you had better watch your step, Jack, or Joe Sedley will be walking off with the prize."

"If Ruth really wants Joe Sedley she can have him," said Jack irritatedly. He was still thinking of the conversation down at the brook.

The boys were standing at a corner of the old farmhouse while speaking, and just as the last remark was made Ruth passed by one of the open windows. She heard Jack's rather ill-advised words and her cheeks flushed deeply. She had been on the point of joining Martha in the sitting room, but now she came to a sudden standstill, bit her lip deeply, and then, looking straight ahead with her cheeks still flaming, marched up to her bedroom, closing the door behind her.

That same day, to add to his worries, Jack received a rather formal note from Joe Sedley in which the rich young man stated that he considered the race had been a tie and asked Jack to set a date for riding it over again. Jack immediately showed the letter to his cousins.

"I wouldn't do it!" said Randy quickly. "Why, if you agreed to that it would tend to show that you were not willing to back up the judges of the contest. They gave the race to you."

"Tell him to take a walk to the north pole and cool off," was the way Andy expressed himself.

"I don't think I'd notice the communication," put in Fred.

"Oh, I'll have to answer it," said Jack, and a little later he addressed a note in reply to Joe Sedley's stating that he would abide by the decision of the judges, and as a consequence that race could not be ridden again. However, if Sedley wanted another contest, Jack would be willing to arrange for it as soon as he returned from the outing he was going to take with his cousins and their visitors.

To this Sedley said abruptly: "It is the first race or nothing. I shall always claim it was a tie." And there the unfortunate incident rested.

CHAPTER VIII
OFF ON AN OUTING

"Now for a good old-fashioned outing in the woods! Boys, we ought to have a bully time!"

It was Gif who spoke, two days later. The boys had seen the girls off on the train at Oak Run across the river from Dexter's Corners and were returning to the farm. He was running one car while Randy was running the other.

The leave-taking at the last minute had been rather hurried, for the reason that the train was coming in when they arrived. Consequently Jack had had little opportunity to speak to Ruth. Previous to the coming away she had held somewhat aloof from him, and for some reason he could not fathom she had not seemed to care whether he came after her or not.

This was exactly opposite to the situation between Fred and Spouter's cousin. May and Fred were seen together nearly all the time, and all of the others came to the conclusion that these young folks had some sort of an understanding between them.

"We'll have a fine time if the weather holds good," said Randy. "But deliver me from an outing up in those woods if it rains for several days."

"Oh, see here, don't be a wet blanket so soon!" cried his twin. "It's not going to rain for a month. I bribed the weather man to hold off."

The boys had already decided on where they were going—to a regular hunting lodge in the woods—and what they would take along. Back of the farm was a swiftly flowing river upon which at one point was located Hump-back Falls. Beyond this were wide stretches of woodland containing not a few small streams flowing into the river. Here the boys had often gone hunting and fishing.

"We can't do much in the way of hunting," declared Jack. "Nearly everything is out of season. Of course you might get a crow, or something like that. But who wants a crow, anyway?"

"I'd like to haul in a good mess of trout," said Gif wistfully.

While at Dexter's Corners and at the railroad station the boys had made a number of inquiries concerning Slugger Brown and Nappy Martell, but obtained no trace of these unworthies. Now in the pleasure of getting ready for their outing their former enemies were forgotten.

"I'll tell you what we might do," said Randy, while they were packing their things. "Why can't we do some real hunting with our cameras? We might get some dandy pictures of wild animals and other subjects."

"That suits me," came from Gif. "I've got a brand-new camera with me, and I'd like first rate to snap something worth while."

"How about a fifteen-foot snake with three knots in his little tail?" suggested Andy.

"No! If I snap a snake I want nothing less than a two-headed anaconda!" was the merry reply. "One that has a couple of humps on his back like a camel."

"What's the matter with taking a picture of some butterfly eggs?" asked Fred.

"No, I want a snapshot of a caterpillar resting on a pillow against a pillar," finished Jack, and then there was a general laugh.

The next day dawned clear and warm and the boys were up for an early breakfast. Each had donned a regular hiking costume, and each carried his stuff in a roll in regular military fashion. They had reduced their stores to a minimum, knowing that they could easily hike over to one of the nearby villages if they happened to run short of provisions.

"Going out to shoot elephants, eh?" was Grandfather Rover's comment, as he stood up on rather shaky legs to bid them good-bye. "Well, don't blow your heads off. You'll need them trying to find your way back."

"If we see any elephants I'll bring a trunk back for you!" cried Andy. "A trunk full of assorted sneezes."

"Don't get shot, any of you," admonished Aunt Martha. "And be careful and don't fall in the river. Just remember that when he was a boy Fred's father nearly lost his life at Humpback Falls."

"And don't get lost in the woods," added Uncle Randolph. "Have you a compass with you?"

"Yes, we've got a compass, Uncle Randolph," said Jack. "And we won't get lost, either. We've been through those woods hundreds of times."

"Sorry you can't shoot no rabbits dis time o' year," remarked Aleck Pop, when the boys were leaving. "You mought brung me home a few more rabbits' foots jest fur luck."

"Oh, we'll bring you a buskarora, Aleck!" exclaimed Andy.

"A buskarora! What's dat? Some new kind of animal?"

"A buskarora, Aleck, is a second cousin to a three-armed jaspinilla," said Andy soberly. "They live in caves with jusjupacks and rusbunions."

"Rusbunions! Is dat something like my own bunions?" asked the colored man.

"Almost, but entirely different. We'll bring you a couple of pounds or two or three feet of them—just as you prefer."

"Don't you brung nothing like dat around me, Andy Rover. Sech strange t'ings might bite. By golly, ain't it wonderful what dem boys learn when dey goes to school? I suppose dem high-soundin' names don't mean nothing but bullfrogs or tadpoles and sech things," and the old colored man shuffled off shaking his head thoughtfully.

It did not take the boys long to reach the river, and they walked along until they found a good fording place and here took off their shoes and sport stockings and waded across.

"If we weren't so anxious to get along, I'd say we might go in swimming," suggested Fred.

"Oh, there are plenty of good places to swim besides this," said Randy. "Let's wait until we get up near the old spring."

On such a hot day it was a relief to get in the woods. Mile after mile was covered, Jack and Randy leading the way and the others close behind. Here and there, climbing over and around the rocks was more or less difficult and once Spouter missed his footing and rolled over and over, to bring up in a tangle of brushwood.

"Hi! Somebody give me a hand!" he yelled. "I'm all tangled up down here!" And then the others had considerable difficulty in getting him out of his predicament without ruining his clothing and the outfit he carried.

By noon they had covered eight or nine miles and came to rest at a small opening where was located the spring that had been mentioned. Here there was a large pool of water, and the boys took a short swim before sitting down to eat.

"Jimminy beeswax!" chattered Fred, after plunging in. "Who said this was a hot bath? It's as cold as Greenland's icy fountains!"

The boys took their time over their lunch, and it was after two o'clock when they resumed their hike. So far they had seen little or no game except some birds and had not attempted to do any shooting.

"Look! See the chipmunks!" cried Fred presently, and pointed to a fallen tree some distance ahead. There were five chipmunks having a merry time running in and out of the tree, which chanced to be hollow.

"There's a snapshot worth getting," announced Gif. "Come on! Let's see what we can do."

All were willing, and, throwing down their loads, they got out their cameras and were soon crawling cautiously towards the tree trunk. Then they prepared to snap their pictures, but just as they were ready the chipmunks took alarm and disappeared as if by magic.

"Sold!" cried Randy, in disgust. "A fine bunch of photographers we are!"

"We should have carried our cameras ready for use. Then we might have got some fine snapshots," said Spouter.

They advanced upon the tree trunk and looked all around that vicinity, but if the chipmunks were anywhere near they did not show themselves. So presently, with nothing else to do, the boys continued on their way. The Rovers knew of a good-sized shack several miles farther on, and there they thought they might rest for the first night out.

A little farther on they came rather unexpectedly upon a roadway, and here was located a fair-sized clearing where a man ran a small farm. As they came closer they heard a woman calling out shrilly.

"Tommy! The crows are after those little chickens again! Run and chase 'em away—quick! Oh, dear, with all those crows around we can't raise anything any more!" And then a red-headed boy appeared, waving a gingham apron in his hand.

The Rover boys and their chums looked up and only a short distance away saw a large flock of crows circling over one side of the farm where were located several chicken houses. On the ground were a number of little chicks, and the crows were evidently after some of these.

"There's our chance! Quick!" yelled Jack, and without further ado he unslung his gun.

The others understood, and all waited until each had his firearm ready for use. In the meantime Fred had run over to the boy and told him to stop waving the apron.

"We'll give those crows something to remember us by," said the youngest of the Rover boys.

"All ready!" yelled Jack. "Take aim!" He paused another instant. "Fire!"

Bang! Crack! Bang! went the guns in almost a perfect volley. The reports were followed by a scream from the woman in the house and a yell of delight from the red-headed boy. Then nine of the crows were seen to be coming down, some dropping rapidly, showing they had been killed instantly, and others fluttering as if badly wounded. With loud caws the other birds wheeled abruptly and flew out of sight.

"That's the time we brought 'em down!" cried Jack, in satisfaction. "Those crows at least won't bother any more chickens."

"Gosh! but you're some hunters, ain't you?" said the red-headed boy, his eyes wide in wonder.

"Oh, that was easy," said Jack. "Come on, fellows, let's go after the birds that we wounded and put them out of their misery."

Three of the crows had been only wounded, and they were quickly dispatched, and then the boys walked back to the farmhouse where they found a lean woman awaiting them.

"You young men certainly came in the nick of time," she declared emphatically. "I'm very much obliged to you, and I'm sure my husband will be too when he gets back from his work. Those crows are the plague of my life. I can't keep the chicks locked up all the time, they need the air and the sunshine. But every time I let 'em out those crows get after them."

"Want them crows?" asked the red-headed boy.

"No. You can have them," said Jack. "But I wouldn't mind having a drink of water," he added.

A well was handy and while the crowd was having a drink the woman continued to talk about her troubles.

"The crows are troubling us all the time, and once in a while we have a tramp or two come here," she vouchsafed. "And yesterday I had two young men stop here and they were just as impudent as they could be."

This remark interested the Rovers and their chums and they immediately asked the woman for some particulars. She said the two undesirable visitors had lost something on the road and insisted that Tommy help them in hunting for it and then had insisted that she supply them with lunch, asking in anything but a friendly fashion. The two young men had gone off only when Tommy had come in announcing that his father was coming down the road.

"What were the names of those young men?" asked Fred.

"They didn't give their names," said the woman, "but one called the other Nappy and he called the first fellow Slugger."

"Slugger Brown and Nappy Martell again!" exclaimed Randy. "Can you beat it?"

CHAPTER IX
THE CABIN IN THE WOODS

MRS. JANDLE, THE FARM woman, gazed at the Rovers and their chums curiously and they had to explain that Nappy Martell and Slugger Brown had once been their school chums but since that time had gotten into all sorts of trouble with the authorities and it was now supposed that they and their families had lost practically all of their money.

"Well, they didn't look like tramps, I'll say that for 'em," said Mrs. Jandle. "They were quite well dressed and they offered to pay for their lunch. But I didn't let 'em have anything, because, as I said before, I didn't like their manner. They were very overbearing."

"And they always were," said Jack. "If they come and annoy you again tell them that you know all about them and that you will have them placed under arrest and that the folks at Valley Brook Farm will appear against them. I'll warrant that will make them clear out in a hurry."

A little later the boys continued in the direction of the place where they intended to spend the night. A part of the road was rough and they had covered less than a mile when Fred called a halt.

"I've got something in my shoe and I want to find out what it is," he announced.

The spot was close to a road that ran through the woods and over a small hill. Looking around, Randy spied several squirrels running up and down a tree trunk and went in that direction to take several snapshots of them.

"I don't like to discourage you fellows," announced Spouter presently. "But if I am any sort of weather prophet, we're going to have a storm, and that very soon."

"The sky certainly does begin to look queer," said Jack after a long look around. "But the storm may pass off to the westward of us."

"I hope we don't get it—at least, not if it's a thunderstorm," came from Spouter. "You all know how dangerous those are."

"You bet we do!" cried Andy. "All of us have been caught out in them more than once."

Having cleared his shoes of the stone which in some way had gotten into it, Fred announced that he was ready to go on and all took up their loads again and marched to the top of the hill, a distance of less than a quarter of a mile. By this time a brisk breeze had sprung up, rustling the bushes and the boughs of the trees, and now the gathering clouds spread over the face of the sun, making the outlook much darker.

"That storm is coming, all right enough," declared Randy.

"Right-o!" added Fred. "Here are the first drops now!" and he put out his hand to verify his words.

"Raindrops as big as quarters!" shouted Gif. "Boys, I'm afraid we're in for a soaking unless we get under some kind of shelter."

"Well, I'm not in favor of standing under the trees," said Spouter. "Not if there is any lightning coming."

He had scarcely spoken when the sky at a distance was illumined, and a few seconds later came the low rumble of thunder. Then the wind gradually increased and the rain came down steadily.

"I guess we're in for it," announced Jack, shaking his head dubiously. "I don't know of a single shelter in this locality."

"Well, then, let's take a double one if we can't find a single one," said Andy, bound to have his little joke.

"If I remember rightly, there is some sort of an old cabin down at the foot of the hill," said Fred. "Don't you remember it, Randy? We stopped there once when we were out nutting a couple of years ago—the time we thought we heard an aëroplane."

"Oh, yes, Fred! I remember that," cried his cousin quickly. "It's right down on the left of the road at the very foot of the hill. Come on, let's run for it before the storm gets too bad."

All were willing to do anything to get under shelter, and they broke into a run, making their way down the hill as rapidly as their outfits permitted.

They were less than half way down the hill when a vivid flash of lightning illumined the sky, followed almost instantly by a loud crack of thunder. All of the boys dodged instinctively and a moment later heard another crash behind them.

"Look! Look!" gasped Jack, turning around. All did so and were just in time to see a tall tree about a hundred yards away fall slowly from the edge of the forest, landing in such a position that it partly blocked the roadway.

"Gee! what do you know about that?" panted Andy, his eyes almost starting from his head. "Why, we came past that spot less than a minute ago!"

"A—a—narrow escape, I'll tell the world!" spluttered Fred. "Come on, let's get to that cabin! It will be at least some safer than being in the open."

By the time the Rovers and their chums gained the foot of the hill the rain was coming down in torrents. The wind was also rising, blowing leaves and small tree branches in various directions. Fred and Randy led the way, leaving the highway at a point where there were a number of large rocks. They stepped over a broken-down wire fence and then ran along a footpath, one side of which was overhung by dense bushes now becoming soaked from the rain.

"Wow!" spluttered Gif presently, as he followed Spouter. His chum had pushed back a large branch of a bush and this now swept back into place, catching Gif full in the face and giving him a perfect shower bath.

"Sorry. But I had to get past somehow," cried Spouter.

"How much farther to go?" demanded Andy.

"Not much farther," said Fred. "I only hope the old cabin hasn't fallen down since Randy and I were here before."

Presently, just as there came more lightning and thunder, those in advance turned a corner of the path and came to a small clearing. In the center of this was on old and dilapidated cabin built, evidently, years before by some lumbermen. The front door to the cabin stood partly open and one of the windows was minus both the sash and the shutter it had once boasted.

"Anybody around?" sang out Jack.

"Don't see anybody," said Fred, and shoved the door still farther back. Then he plunged into the cabin and one after another the others followed.

If the outside of the place looked dilapidated, the inside was just as bad if not worse. The floor was thick with dirt and so were the walls, and in the upper part a number of birds circled around wildly in an endeavor to get out by way of several small openings.

"Not much of a place to stay in, but a whole lot better than nothing," was the way Gif expressed himself.

"Perhaps we'll have to stay here all night," remarked Jack, as he shook the water from his cap.

"I hope no tree comes down and hits this place," remarked Randy. "A good big tree could knock this cabin as flat as a pancake and leave us under the ruins."

"You're a cheerful bird, I don't think," said Spouter. "Just the same, I don't think there is any danger of a tree hitting the cabin. All the big ones around here have been cut off and the second growth doesn't amount to much."

The boys stacked their outfits in the middle of the floor where only a few drops of rain could get at them and then stood by the broken-out window and the doorway looking at the storm. Fortunately the rain was driving from the rear of the place, and as this seemed to be more or less tight only a small quantity of water came into the cabin.

"I'd hate to stay in such a rank place as this all night," said Fred, as the downpour continued, punctuated every now and then by flashes of lightning and cracks of thunder. "But what are we going to do if this storm keeps up?"

"Oh, it may stop before night comes on," said Jack. "Anyway, we're simply out for sport, so we might as well make the best of what comes," and he smiled grimly.

Presently the lightning and thunder seemed to die away and the fury of the sudden storm abated. Yet the rain came down steadily and the boys felt it would be foolish to try to go farther until there was more of a let-up.

"We'd get wet to the skin in no time and all of our outfit would get wet, too," said Jack. "We may as well content ourselves here."

Getting somewhat tired of standing straight up watching the storm, the boys began to move around the deserted cabin. They found the lower floor consisted of four rooms, one evidently having been used for a kitchen, another for a messroom, and the other two for sleeping quarters. In the latter rooms there were a number of rough bunks against the walls, some still containing straw and other material used for bedding.

"I wouldn't bunk in one of those places for a farm," said Fred to Andy. "I'll bet they're full of vermin."

"Looks to me like a dandy place for snakes," was Andy's answer. "I'll wager there are plenty of snakes under the flooring of this building."

Once or twice the boys had heard some strange sounds not unlike the barking of young dogs. On account of the thunder and the noise made by the falling rain, they had not been able to trace these sounds and had thought they must come from a distance.

"Listen!" cried Jack presently. "Do I hear a dog?"

"Sounds like a terrier," said Gif. "But I don't know where he is."

Having poked around the cabin, Andy and Fred pushed open a door in what had been the kitchen of the cabin. Here there was a lean-to meant for a pantry, and beyond this another small structure evidently intended for the housing of firewood.

"Beeswax and onions!" exclaimed Andy presently. "Look here, fellows! What do you make of this?" He pointed from a doorway of the pantry which led into the woodshed. He had a flashlight in his hand, and this he now played on a large box in a corner of the shed. Here in a pile of rubbish were several small animals, all barking in a peculiar fashion.

"What are they—dogs?" asked Spouter, coming up.

"Dogs nothing!" cried Fred. "Don't you know what they are? Foxes!"

"That's what they are," said Jack, giving a careful look. "Some old mother fox has been using this corner for her den."

"Say, if that's so, we'd better look out for the mother fox!" exclaimed Randy, in alarm. "No wild animal will allow any one to molest her young without a fight."

"Yes, and a stiff fight, too!" added Gif.

Gif had scarcely spoken when there was a wild barking and snapping outside of the old cabin. Then came a sudden leap through a wide-open window and the next instant the six boys found themselves confronted by a full-sized and very angry looking mother fox.

CHAPTER X
AN UNEXPECTED BLAZE

FOR THE INSTANT THE six boys were so startled that they knew not what to do. None of them was armed, their firearms and their fishing outfits resting on the floor with their rolls.

But if the lads were taken aback, so was the mother fox. She had landed squarely on the floor and now shrank back, hair bristling on end and her eyes staring wildly at what was before her. Astonishment seemed to give way to fear over the welfare of her offspring and then her eyes gleamed with a sudden ferocity. Had there been no young ones she might have leaped through the window again for safety, but now she would fight to the death for those she loved.

"Come on! Get out of here!" yelled Jack, catching Fred by the arm.

"If I only had a gun!" came from Spouter.

"Come to the door, I tell you, and leave that fox alone!" went on Jack.

"She wants to get at her young ones—that's what she wants!" burst out Randy.

"Well, she can have her kids for all I care," said his twin. "Me for the open spaces," and he followed Jack and Fred through one room to another and then outside, and the others came swiftly upon their heels.

Twice the mother fox barked and showed her teeth viciously, but at the same time she backed around in a semicircle and a few seconds later slunk out of sight through a hole in the back wall of the cabin.

"She's after her little ones, all right enough," said Jack. "Probably there is another hole leading into the woodshed from the outside."

"We'd better arm ourselves while we've got the chance," said Randy. "There's no telling what that old fox may start to do."

"I don't think I want to kill her," said Fred. "If you did that, you'd have to kill her young ones too."

The boys were now standing in a group in the rain, not knowing what to do next. Presently Jack and Gif walked around one side of the cabin. They were just in time to see the nose of the fox disappearing from a small hole in the side of the woodshed.

"She's in there all right enough," said Gif.

"And she can stay there for all of me," said Jack. "I suppose it would be the proper thing to kill that fox and also her young. But somehow, after looking at the little things, I haven't got the heart to do it."

Jack and Gif joined the others and found that they had brought forth from the cabin all the firearms the party carried.

"An old mother fox like that can make a lot of trouble for a farmer's chickens," said Gif. "Really more trouble than the crows. She ought to be slaughtered and the young ones ought to be slaughtered too."

"Well, do you want to do the slaughtering, Gif?" asked Fred quickly. "I declare I don't."

"Well, I—er—I think it ought to be done," stammered the youth who had been at the head of the Colby Hall Athletic Association.

"All right then, we'll appoint you the head of the committee to do the deed," declared Spouter.

"Well, what do you say about it?" demanded Gif.

"I'll say that it's something that really ought to be done for the benefit of society at large," declared Spouter. "Foxes commit all sorts of depredations and everybody knows they forfeit their lives a dozen times or more a year. Besides that, fox skins are valuable. At the same time—" and here Spouter paused. "At the same time, so far as I am concerned that old mother fox can live to take care of her little family."

"And thus doth the judge render his decision in this court," quoted Andy solemnly. "Gentlemen of the jury, what is your verdict?"

The verdict was unanimous that a fox was a rascal and a thief and ought to be killed on general principles, but as there was no one on hand who was willing to commit the deed the fox was to go unmolested.

The rain was still coming down steadily, and, not to get soaked, the boys stepped rather gingerly into the living room of the old cabin. Then, with great caution, they closed the doors leading to the other rooms.

"Now if that old fox wants to get at us she'll have to come around to the front of the building," said Jack.

"Gosh! what a grand picture that old fox and her young ones would make," sighed Fred. "I wish we had had a chance to get a picture of the little ones before the mother hove in sight."

"Well, you be thankful, Fred, that you didn't get a sample of her teeth in the calf of your leg," said Randy. "If she ever started on a rampage I bet she'd be worse than a wildcat."

Looking from the cabin, the boys saw that the storm was passing. Here and there the blue sky was showing, and presently the rain stopped falling and they saw a bit of sunshine drift across the water-soaked trees and bushes.

"We might as well be going," declared Jack. "You know these storms have a way of working around and coming back, and we want to make that hunters' lodge before night if we possibly can."

"I'd like to get another look at that old fox," declared Fred, as he adjusted his roll.

"Nothing doing!" declared Jack. "You leave well enough alone. Don't you remember that old story about Larry Duncan? He went into a fox's den and one of the old timers jumped up and just about bit off his nose. You'd look fine with half your nose missing!"

"Oh, come on—I was only fooling," said the youngest Rover boy.

In a short while they had left the old cabin and were once more on the road. For over half a mile they had to slosh along through the mud and water, but after that they came to a stony trail where going was considerably better. The stop at the cabin had rested them, and they made good progress during the last two miles of the hike.

"Hurrah! The sun is coming out!" cried Gif presently. "I think we've seen the last of that storm."

Randy and Spouter were in advance and presently they set up a shout as they came in sight of the little hunters' lodge for which the party was bound. This place belonged to a couple of gentlemen living near Dexter's Corners and they often allowed the Rovers and others to use it.

When they arrived at the place the boys found the door locked and all the wooden shutters over the windows in place. Jack had the key and they soon opened up. Then while Fred and Andy started the fire on the hearth of the broad stone chimney the others opened the windows and placed the lodge in order generally.

"We'll have to dry out our clothing first of all," declared Gif. "It's lucky we brought extra knickers along in our rolls."

"Yes, and then I'll want something to eat!" declared Andy. "Gee, I'm almost hungry enough to chew nails!"

"That's your reason for hurrying up with the fire, I guess," grinned Jack. "Well, go to it! The sooner we dry out and get something to eat, the sooner we'll feel at home."

The others were getting some of the provisions from their outfits when Fred and Andy, who were coaxing the fire, suddenly let out a yell of alarm.

"What's the matter with the chimney?"

"Looks to me as if it was on fire!"

"Hi! what's that?" exclaimed Spouter. "You certainly don't want to burn this place up!"

There was a strange roaring of flames in the chimney, then, of a sudden, a back draft sent the smoke and the sparks out into the room and into the faces of the boys. They stumbled back wildly, several to the open windows and the others to the doorway.

"I know what's the matter!" exclaimed Fred. "It's birds' nests! They had the same trouble several years ago. Mr. Randolph was telling me about it."

"Well, what did they do about it?" demanded Jack quickly.

"Got up on the roof and put it out with a couple of pails of water," was the reply.

"Gee, it's a wonder the stuff isn't too wet to burn," remarked Gif. "We've had rain enough."

"Let's get water and be quick about it," came from Jack. "Even if the chimney is a substantial one the sparks may set the roof on fire."

The hunters' lodge was comfortably furnished, and the boys had already noted a couple of tin pails in the kitchen pantry.

"I know where the spring is!" cried Fred. "Hurry up!"

"How are we going to get up on the roof?"

"There's a permanent ladder in the back of the lodge," was the reply. "And there are foot cleats leading up to the chimney."

Grabbing up not only the pails but also several pots and a teakettle, the boys rushed after Fred down to where a spring bubbled up between the rocks. Here there was a small pool of cool, clear water which they proceeded to scoop up as rapidly as possible. Then they rushed to the rear of the lodge and Jack was the first to mount the ladder which was nailed beside a rear window. He carried a pail of water in one hand and behind him came Randy with the second pail and Spouter with the teakettle. The boys had worked as quickly as possible, but many precious seconds had been lost and the fire in the chimney was now roaring merrily, the flames shooting several feet above the top and carrying the sparks in all directions.

"My gracious, that roof will catch, as sure as shooting!" gasped Fred. "Just look at those sparks, will you?"

Balancing himself as best he could with the pail of water, Jack mounted the sloping roof of the lodge until he came within a few feet of the chimney. The sparks fell all around him, some even landing on his cap and clothing. Then he let fly with the contents of the pail and more than three-quarters of the water went down into the chimney.

"Hurrah, that's the way to do it!" came encouragingly from Gif. "Throw the pail down, Jack!"

This was done, and then Randy passed the second pail along and this was followed by the teakettle.

"Go inside and see that the fire doesn't scatter around the room," yelled the oldest Rover boy, as the contents of the teakettle followed the second pail of water into the chimney.

Andy did as bidden and at the same time Gif with the two pails hurried off once more to the spring. Inside of the lodge there was a dense smoke and a little trickle of water came from the hearthstone across the floor. This carried with it some ashes and a few bits of wood and straw.

The first supply of water was soon exhausted and by the time a fresh quantity came up from the spring the fire in the chimney was again belching forth, sending out almost as many sparks as ever.

"Lively there, boys! Lively!" yelled Jack, brushing the sparks from his face and hands.

"Here you are!" yelled Gif. "Pass 'em along!" and one pail after another came up.

"The roof is on fire!" screamed Spouter. "Here, give me that teakettle of water!"

Spouter was right. The sparks had set fire to the roof in several places. He crawled forward as well as the slippery condition of the shingles permitted. Then, with the water, he put out one of the blazes and immediately crawled off in the direction of another.

"Be careful there!" cried Gif. "Throw down the pails again and I'll get more water."

"Gosh! this is worse than I thought it was going to be," groaned Randy. "I thought a pail or two of water would put it all out!"

"Hi! Hi! Take care there!" came suddenly from Gif.

He was yelling at Spouter whose left foot had slipped from under him. Then came a yell of fright, and the next moment Spouter dropped the teakettle with a clatter and rolled over and over and shot from the roof of the lodge to the ground below!

CHAPTER XI
WHAT HAPPENED ON THE ROAD

BOTH JACK AND RANDY were greatly alarmed when they saw their former school chum roll from the roof of the hunters' lodge and disappear from sight.

"He'll break his neck!" gasped Randy.

Andy was on the ladder with a pot of water when the accident occurred. He saw Spouter fly over the edge of the roof, turn something of a somersault and then come down very much in the shape of a huge frog. He landed in some low bushes growing beside a window, and then fell backward on the wet grass.

"Spouter!" exclaimed Gif, rushing up, followed by Fred. "Are you hurt?"

There was no immediate answer to this, but the boy who loved occasionally to orate turned over slowly on his hands and knees and then got up on his feet.

"Gee, what a tumble!" came from Fred. "Are you sure you're all right, Spouter?"

"I—I—guess so," panted the unfortunate one. "Gee, but I came down awfully sudden like, didn't I?" he added, rubbing his shoulder and then his hip.

Under ordinary circumstances all of the other boys would have paid more attention to Spouter. But now, when they saw he was not seriously injured, they immediately turned their attention again to the fire.

Pail after pail of water was taken to the roof, and gradually the flames in the chimney subsided and then went out altogether. The last few pailfuls were thrown by Randy, for Jack was almost exhausted, so strenuously had he labored to put out the conflagration.

While the work was going on overhead Fred, followed by Spouter, had reëntered the lodge and they were busy cleaning up the muss on the hearth and on the floor. Spouter limped a little, but refused to take care of his bruises until all were assured that the fire was a thing of the past.

"We were lucky to get it out so easily," declared Jack. "At one time I thought sure the whole roof would catch fire." He and Randy had extinguished the flames on the shingles which Spouter had been fighting.

"I don't know what the owners of the lodge will say to this," remarked Randy, as he looked at the muss on the floor. "But I don't think they can claim that the fire in the chimney was our fault."

"I can't understand how a few birds' nests could make such an awful blaze as that," declared Jack. "The chimney went off as if it was stuffed with wood."

Later on the boys solved the mystery of the fire. During some previous storm a long branch of a tree had been blown to the roof of the lodge and then settled down into the chimney. Here it had had time to dry and in it the birds had established their nests. Thus when the fire was started on the hearth the dried-out limb with its dead leaves and birds' nests had acted very much like a huge torch.

It was not until two hours later that the boys had cleaned up the muss. They examined the chimney carefully and it was cleaned out thoroughly so that no more fires of that sort might occur. Then they started another blaze and prepared supper, after which all of them felt better, even though Spouter complained somewhat of a bruise on his shoulder and another on his hip and Jack and Randy exhibited several places on their hands and necks where the sparks had touched them.

As has been said, the lodge was well furnished and that night the boys slept almost as comfortably as if they had been at home. They left a low fire burning so that their garments might dry out and none of them stirred until the sun was well up in the heavens.

"No use of going on an outing if you can't take your time about it," remarked Gif, as he arose and stretched himself.

"Let's be thankful we're not in an encampment at Colby Hall," said Andy. "If we were, Major Jack would have us all up at daybreak and on the parade ground," and he grinned at his cousin.

"Attention!" came suddenly from the former major of the Colby Hall battalion, and, taken off their guard, Andy, Randy and Spouter leaped up and stood as straight as ramrods. Then came a burst of laughter from Jack and the others, and even the victims of his little joke could not help but join in.

The various happenings of the day before had tired all of the lads, and they were perfectly content to take it easy that day. The sun came out warmly and soon all traces of the storm had passed. The boys lolled around in the sun or in the shade as suited them, resting and telling stories.

"I wish I knew what had brought Slugger Brown and Nappy Martell to this neighborhood," remarked Jack. "I'm sure they wouldn't come up here excepting for some especial purpose."

"It certainly is queer that Slugger looked in at your window," said Spouter. "He's a bad egg. You'd better keep your eyes peeled for him."

"And then to think they stopped at that farmhouse where we shot the crows," put in Fred. "That shows that they can't be so very far from this neighborhood."

"Maybe they'll try some such game as the Davenport crowd did," suggested Spouter. "You'd feel fine if you were kidnapped again, wouldn't you, Jack?"

"Well, we got the best of the Davenport crowd," said the former major of the Colby Hall battalion. "Maybe we could get ahead of Slugger and his bunch too, not to say anything of that sneak, Nappy Martell."

Not a great distance back of the hunters' lodge was located a small river and a fair-sized lake. Here the lads thought they might have luck fishing and the next day set off for this sport after a late breakfast. They took their lunch with them, not knowing how soon they would come back.

Fishing along the river was not particularly successful, although Randy and Gif did manage to land two small trout. Then they reached the lake and here had a little better success, getting two more trout and a dozen perch, as well as a number of catfish.

"I'm tired of fishing," said Randy, after he had four specimens of the finny tribe to his credit. "I'm going to put up my rod and see what I can find to shoot with the camera."

The others wished to continue the sport, so Randy went off by himself, following the lake-shore for a short distance and then moving away to where a fairly well constructed roadway ran along one side of the water.

This was after the boys had partaken of their lunch, and now the others continued their fishing for an hour longer. But there was little more success and finally one after another reeled in his line and put away his rod.

"Wonder where Randy went to?" asked Fred presently.

"Oh, I don't think he's very far off," said Jack.

"I'll give him a call and find out," put in Andy, and, placing his two little fingers in the corners of his mouth, he gave what was called a locomotive whistle—something he had learned from his father, the old whistle that Tom Rover had made so popular at Putnam Hall.

After the whistle all listened intently and from a considerable distance came two whistles in return. Then Andy whistled four times to signal to his twin that they were ready to go back, and immediately came three whistles from Randy to show that he understood.

"I wonder if he got any pictures worth taking," mused Fred. He was disappointed that he had not gone along, having brought his own camera with him.

"Never mind, Fred. Here! we'll all stand in a row holding up our catches and you can snap that for a picture," suggested Andy, and this was done.

"We should have stood about ten feet from the camera and held out our fish directly in front of us," suggested Spouter. "Then the fish would look about three times bigger than they are," and at this there was a general snicker.

Having taken several other pictures, the boys prepared to leave the place and again Andy whistled for his twin. This time, however, there was no reply.

"That's funny," remarked Gif. "He's supposed to answer, isn't he, Andy?"

"Sure."

"Maybe he doesn't want to make any noise," suggested Fred. "He may be trying to get a picture of some birds or squirrels, or something like that. And if he made a noise he'd scare them away."

"You may be right," said Jack. "Well, all we can do is to hang around and wait for him to come. We're in no hurry, anyway."

The boys moved forward slowly, walking in the direction of the roadway just mentioned. Andy was in advance, swinging his small catch of fish from a twig as he moved along.

"Let's wake Randy up with the old school song!" cried Gif, and then began as loudly as he could, with all of the others joining in:

> "Who are we?
> Can't you see?
> Colby Hall!
> Dum, dum! dum, dum, dum!
> Here we come with fife and drum!
> Colby, Colby, Colby Hall!"

This they repeated twice and then added the old baseball refrain, that refrain which had often brought them success in the games against Hixley High, Longley Academy, and other rival institutions.

> "We've got the goods! We've got the goods!
> Because we played good ball.
> No matter what we try to do,
> Old Colby's got the call!"

"Gee, sounds like a touch of old times!" said Jack. "Wouldn't you like to be on the ballfield at the Hall to-day?"

"Indeed I would!" said Gif, his eyes glistening. "How we would knock the stuffing out of Tommy Flanders and his bunch!"

"I'll tell you, those days at Colby Hall were certainly great!" put in Spouter wistfully. "No matter what happens to me, I don't believe I'll ever forget the many good times we had at that school. And I'll never forget what a good sport Colonel Colby always was!"

"Never a better man!" declared Fred. "And never a better school. It's too bad we had to graduate. I'd like to go back for another year or two."

"Wow! Listen to him, will you?" exclaimed Jack. "Did you ever hear the like! A fellow wanting to go back to school!"

"I'll bet you'd like to go back yourself, Jack," was the quick retort.

"So I would! But not to do any studying. I'd like to be on the ballfield for a game or two, and I'd like to be in command of the battalion during a drill and a parade, and maybe for a week or two in camp. But no more school books, thank you!"

"Oh, well, let's forget it!" cried Fred, and then, with a sly look at his oldest cousin, he began to hum softly:

"Down on the ocean bottom, boys;
Down on the ocean bottom!"

"For the love of smoked beef, Fred, why don't you tell us what it's all about?" demanded Jack. "You promised to tell us—you know you did."

"Have patience, old man! Have patience!" returned the youngest Rover solemnly. "The answer is coming soon—have patience."

While talking, the boys had reached the roadway, Andy in advance of the others. Then all heard a noise in the distance and looked up to see what it meant.

"It's an auto, and making some speed," said Gif. "Gee, this is no road to race on!" he added, looking at the uneven highway.

Andy was still well ahead and now he, as well as the others, stepped to the side of the road to let the car pass. On it came and then they noticed that the car, which was large and powerful, had a broken mudguard and that one of the headlights was smashed.

"Look out!" screamed Jack. "Of all the fools—" and then he and those near him had to fall back into some bushes as the big car lurched by within a few inches of them.

"By golly, the fellow running that car ought to be arrested!" gasped Gif. "He must be crazy to run like that."

"Looks to me as if they were running away from some accident," said Jack. "The mudguard and one light were broken."

"Look! Look!" screamed Spouter, pointing up the roadway in the direction which the automobile had taken. "They knocked Andy down! He's lying in the road!"

CHAPTER XII
FRED TELLS HIS STORY

THE OTHERS GAZED IN the direction Spouter pointed out and saw, about a hundred feet away, Andy lying on his face in the rough roadway. As they gazed at him they saw the youth try to rise and then fall over on his back.

"He's hurt!" gasped Fred.

"Yes, and I'm afraid he's hurt pretty badly," returned Jack.

"The skunks who did this ought to be arrested!" cried Gif.

All hurried to where Andy lay. They found him with his eyes closed and breathing heavily. The cadets of the Colby Hall had been well drilled in first-aid to the injured, and while Gif, Jack and Fred carried Andy to a grassy bank by the roadside and looked him over, Spouter sped off in the direction of the lake and presently returned with his cap and a long thermos bottle full of water.

But even though they used the water and chafed Andy's hands, it was a full five minutes before he regained his senses and opened his eyes. Even then he could not collect his thoughts and stared wildly around him.

"It's all right, Andy," said Jack soothingly, as he placed his cousin's head and shoulders against his knees. "The auto knocked you down, but we'll take care of you."

"Did—did—you—you stop the rascals?" mumbled Andy. "They ought to be hung!"

"No, we didn't stop them. We had to jump to save ourselves," said Fred.

A little later Andy felt more like himself, and then he essayed to get to his feet. This was a rather difficult operation and he emitted several groans during the process. The others, however, were glad to learn that neither of his legs was broken or seriously injured.

"The auto hit me in the hip and then when I went down the mudguard or something scraped along my shoulder and my head," he gasped.

"Yes, your ear and your neck have been bleeding," said Jack. "But let's be thankful that no bones are broken."

"Jack, he might have killed me!" and for once the fun-loving Rover looked much disturbed.

"And the worst of it is that we didn't even get the license number," moaned Fred.

"Well, anyway, we know it was an open touring car and that it had the left mudguard and headlight smashed. That looks as if the car had been in a collision before it struck Andy and that the driver was doing his best to get away."

"Well, he was certainly making the engine do all it could," was Gif's comment.

"Gracious, I wonder where Randy is!" exclaimed Jack suddenly.

"If he was out on the road he may have been struck too!" put in Fred.

"Oh! isn't my twin here?" put in Andy, gazing around in bewilderment. "Gee, I'm so fussed up over this knock-down I didn't even miss him! Was he out on the road too?"

"You know as much about that as we do, Andy," said Fred. "The last we heard from him was when you whistled and he said."

"Well, some of you fellows had better look for him. I can't do it just yet—my hip is too sore. I'll sit down here on the grass and rest awhile. Gosh, it will be too bad if they have struck him!"

"The rest of you look for Randy. I'll stay with Andy," said Gif. "I don't think he ought to be left just yet."

"You're right," said Jack. Then he and Fred, as well as Spouter, hurried back on the road in the direction where they thought they might find the missing lad.

Ten minutes later, by calling and whistling, they located Randy while he was taking a picture of a fallen tree and some shapely rocks which had struck his fancy.

"What's the excitement?" he demanded, as they came up and he saw that they were much disturbed.

"A touring car just tore along the roadway and knocked Andy down," said Fred. "We were wondering if it had hit you."

"Andy! Did it hurt him much?"

"It bumped him pretty badly on the hip and scraped his ear and neck," said Jack. "But we're all thankful that he wasn't killed or didn't have some of his bones broken. He's resting back a way on the grass and Gif is with him." Then, at Randy's earnest solicitation, the others gave him the particulars.

"They were a bunch of wild riders, all right enough," declared Randy. "There was a big groundhog out in the road and I was just getting ready to take a snapshot when I heard the auto tearing along. The groundhog sat up to listen and I was just snapping the picture when the auto tore along and I think went right over the animal. But the groundhog limped away and out of sight in the bushes."

"Oh, Randy, then the auto must have swept pretty close to you!" gasped Fred.

"I'll say it did—it wasn't more than four or five feet from me and sailing along to beat the band!"

"Do you think you got a picture of the car?" asked Jack eagerly.

"I don't know. Maybe I did. I know I snapped the shutter of the camera, but I was so excited over the passing of the car that I'm not sure how I had the camera pointed. The fact is, I'm afraid the film was spoiled."

"I hope it wasn't spoiled," said Fred. "It might give us some chances to find out who was in the car and maybe get the number."

"The car looked to me as if it was covered with dirt," said Jack. "And if that's so, then the license plate would be covered with dirt too, so the number wouldn't show."

Randy was anxious to see how badly his twin had been hurt, and the crowd quickly returned to where the injured lad was resting. They found Gif out in the roadway examining the surroundings carefully.

"I've got two bits of evidence that may help," said Gif. "One is that the touring car used two kinds of tires, those with diamond-shaped nubs on one side and L-shaped nubs on the other. And then I picked up this and it looks as if it had just been dropped on the road because, as you can see, it's perfectly clean and dry. If it had been there any length of time it would be wet and dirty."

The object he spoke of was a paper bag which had evidently contained fruit, for it now held several orange and banana skins. The bag was marked with the advertisement of a fruit dealer of Yonkers, N. Y.

"Gracious! if that car came from Yonkers it's more than likely that it came right up from New York City," declared Jack.

Andy was gradually feeling more like himself, yet it was a full hour before the boys attempted to start on the return to the hunting lodge.

"We'll take turns carrying you if you say so," said Jack.

"Sure we can do that!" cried Gif, and the others said the same.

"Oh, I think I can manage it alone," declared Andy. "But of course I can't walk very fast." And so the four Rovers took their time while Gif and Spouter went on ahead to prepare supper for the crowd.

At the lodge the boys had more to work with, and Andy's injuries were carefully washed with warm water and then bathed with witch-hazel.

"I guess I'll have to take it easy to-morrow," declared the suffering boy, as he rested on a comfortable couch. "I suppose I'll be as stiff as a ramrod."

"Oh, well, if you have to stay in the lodge I'll stay with you," said his twin quickly.

"And I'll read to you," put in Fred. "There are a whole lot of interesting books in this place."

"I know what you can do, Fred," and Andy suddenly grinned in spite of the pain he was enduring. "You can tell us the story of the ocean bottom."

"Gee, that's just what he can do!" burst out Randy.

"I'll second the commotion on that!" came from Jack.

"Say, what in the name of striped cauliflower is all this talk about 'ocean bottom'?" demanded Gif.

"Sounds to me as if somebody was going to stake out an underwater city," came from Spouter. "Maybe Fred is going to sell town lots warranted free from malaria and mosquitoes with an extended view of coral highways and a beautifully enameled pool for whales."

"Say, Spouter, I know what business you ought to go into," cried Fred. "You ought to be a real estate agent. You'd make your fortune at it."

"Never mind, Fred. Don't try to switch us from the ocean bottom to real estate," interrupted Jack. "If you want to make Andy feel better you just tell us about this secret you've been carrying on your shoulders so long."

"All right. If I must, I must," said the youngest Rover in mock despair. "I'll spin my little yarn after we've had supper and everything is tidied up."

"Hurrah!" shouted Randy. "Here comes the first volume of Fred's interesting series, entitled 'Down on the Ocean Bottom; or, Looking for the Lost Suspenders.'"

"Say, Fred, if this is a lost treasure you should have told us about it before," said Jack. "Then I could have picked out all of the savings banks in which I should want to place my part of the loot."

"If you're going to make fun of it before I've a chance to say a word, I won't say anything," declared Fred, and tried to look as if he felt much injured.

"Oh, don't pout, little boy," said Spouter. "Be real good and maybe we'll give you an extra gingersnap for dessert."

Even though hurt, Andy managed to eat his full share of the meal which Gif and Spouter had prepared and which consisted largely of the fish the crowd had caught. The others also enjoyed what was set before them, yet it must be confessed that all of the other Rover boys, and also their chums, were curious concerning the revelation Fred might have to make.

"I don't suppose any of you ever heard of Miguel Torra," said Fred, after everything had been put away and the whole crowd were comfortably seated in front of the hunting lodge. "He was a Mexican revolutionist who disappeared many years ago."

"Say, see here, Fred, you promised to tell us about this ocean bottom business!" interrupted Randy.

"So I did. But I can't tell you about the ocean bottom until I get there," was the answer. "This Miguel Torra was not in favor with his government at that time, and neither was he in favor with the United States authorities. In fact, so far as my father has been able to learn, he was little short of being an out-and-out bandit, although a good many of his followers were simply revolutionists."

"All right! Proceed!" put in Andy, as his cousin paused.

"Well, this Torra got together a small amount of cash and also a large amount of jewels and gold and silverware, the results of numerous raids made in various parts of the country and also along the Texan border. Then, when matters got too hot for the rascal and his followers, he journeyed to the sea coast with half a dozen of his closest comrades and either hired or commandeered a small steam yacht called the *Margarita*. There was a fight on the shore and the steam yacht got away somewhat damaged. Then the yacht set sail, either for the West Indies or for the north coast of South America."

"Gee, this begins to sound interesting," declared Jack.

"Don't interrupt Fred!" cried Andy. "He's going along slowly enough as it is."

"I can't give you any of the details of what happened shortly after that because I don't know them," went on the youngest Rover boy. "But I do know there was a row on board the steam yacht and a terrible storm came up and then the crowd tried to get back to land. The *Margarita* was wrecked and everything on board was lost."

"What became of Miguel Torra and his bunch?"

"It is supposed that he and all the others lost their lives. But nobody seems to be sure of that."

"Well, where do we come in on this, Fred?" demanded Randy.

"I'm getting to that," said his cousin. "Did you ever hear my dad speak of old Captain Corning?"

"Seems to me I have," said Jack. "I think your father once made some pretty good investments for the old sea dog."

"That's the man. My father likes him very much and thinks he's very reliable. Well, to cut a long story short, Captain Corning knows all about this affair of the *Margarita* and he's now looking for somebody to finance him so that he can go on a hunt for this missing yacht."

"But if she's at the bottom of the ocean how are you going to get to her?" demanded Jack. "Even the best of the divers find it impossible to get down beyond a certain depth. If they could get down as far as they wanted to, they could raise all sorts of sunken ships and get treasures worth billions."

"Well, I believe that Captain Corning has his own ideas as to where the steam yacht is located. And more than that, I think he has an idea that if the divers can't get down to her in their ordinary outfits they can make use of a newly invented diving bell and reach the *Margarita* that way."

"All very interesting," declared Andy. "But where do we come in?"

"Why, we might come in this way. I say 'might,' because it isn't yet settled," said Fred. "But my father talked it over with me, and he intimated that if the whole scheme looked good to him, he would not only finance Captain Corning's project, but he might also join the expedition that went hunting for the lost steam yacht, and, in that case, he might take us fellows along."

CHAPTER XIII
STARTLING NEWS

"Hurrah for Uncle Sam!"

"How long before we could start, do you think, Fred?"

"A trip to the ocean would just suit me!"

Such were the remarks from the three other Rover boys after they had listened to what Fred had to tell about Captain Corning's project and what his parent might do concerning it.

"Say, Fred, do we come in on this?" asked Gif.

"I don't think I could go," added Spouter sorrowfully. "I'm booked for a trip to the coast of Maine. And, incidentally, Gif, I thought you were going with me."

"I'm sorry, Gif, but I'm afraid we'd have to leave you behind," said the youngest Rover boy. "It's too bad, but when my father first talked about it, he spoke of taking me and nobody else. But when he said that, I told him he'd have to take my cousins or I wouldn't go."

"Gee, Fred, it was all right of you to do that!" put in Randy admiringly.

"Well, if I can't go, I can't, and that's all there is to it," remarked Gif. "And maybe Spouter and I will have a real good time up on the Maine coast. Anyway, I hope so."

"How soon do you think we'll find out for certain about this trip?" asked Andy.

"Oh, I expect to know very soon," said his cousin. "The fact is, I've been holding off expecting every day either to get a letter from my dad or have him come up to the farm in person. That's why I didn't want to say anything before this. I wanted to be sure of what I was doing. Even as it is, the whole thing may fall through—and if it does, please don't blame me."

"We won't blame you, Fred. You can be sure of that," returned Jack. "We know you'll be just as much disappointed as any of us. Just the same, I shouldn't want Uncle Sam to put a lot of money in this expedition if the whole thing was a fake. It will cost a pile of dollars to put such a thing through."

"I don't think I'd go into that if I was your father until I had gone over this Captain Corning's information very carefully," remarked Spouter. "There are thousands of people all over this country who think they have special information concerning lost treasure ships and lost mines and lost everything else, and nine out of ten of these things are fakes pure and simple. I remember reading in an old magazine how miles and miles of coast line on Long Island and on Cape Cod had been dug up by people looking for pirates' gold, and how they had even gone up into Newfoundland and down on the Brazil coast and down in Florida, not to say anything of the West Indies, and hunted over miles and miles of all sorts of territory. And then down in Central America and off the coast of Brazil and off the coast of Africa, too, there have been expeditions—"

"Hurrah, Spouter is giving us a lecture on Pirates' Treasures!" burst in Jack gayly. "Why didn't you hand it in as a theme when we were at good old Colby, Spouter? You might have gotten one hundred and one per cent. on it."

"Oh, say! you make me forget what I was talking about," was the reply. "Just the same, as I said before, this treasure game is a good deal of a fake."

"Well, anyway, we'll have a dandy outing if we start looking for that lost *Margarita*," came from Fred.

"We mustn't forget that our folks went on a treasure hunt once before," announced Jack. "They went down to an island in the West Indies looking for a lost treasure that belonged to my mother and her family," he concluded, referring to an affair which has been related in detail in the volume entitled, "The Rover Boys on Treasure Isle; or, The Strange Cruise of the Steam Yacht."

The boys continued to talk about the treasure until it was time to turn in. Fred, however, could give but few more details and he and his cousins hoped that Fred's father would soon announce what he proposed to do.

"I'd like to go on a trip like that before I settle down in business," said Jack, and his youngest cousin agreed with him.

In spite of the witch-hazel and the liniment he used that night, Andy felt stiff and lame the next morning and was quite content to stay around the lodge for all of that day. Fred and Randy remained with him, Jack going off with Gif and Spouter to do some hunting and fishing.

"I wish I had the necessary materials at hand so that I could develop those pictures I snapped," said Randy when the others were gone. "Then I'd find out whether I'd got a picture of that auto or not."

"I hope you did get a picture, and that it proves to be just as clear as the one Ruth took of the horse race," returned Andy. "I'd like to get that fellow's number and then go and report him."

"I don't think it was the car run by Slugger Brown and Nappy Martell," said Fred.

"No, it was a different machine. But that doesn't say those fellows might not have been in it."

While Andy took it easy in a hammock under the trees his brother and Fred put the lodge in order, for the boys knew that the owners of the place would expect them to do this.

"We won't be able to stay here much longer," said Fred. "Because I know that in a few days at the most Gif and Spouter will want to be on their way."

"Yes, and we'll want to hear from Uncle Sam now that we know what is on the carpet," returned Randy.

The other boys tramped quite a few miles that day, and while they had little success in hunting they fared better when it came to fishing. They had seen two foxes and had opened fire on the animals, but without success. They had, however, brought down several good-sized squirrels and been able to pull up eight fair-sized perch and quite a few catfish, as well as several other fish which they could not name.

"The fish suit me," remarked Jack, as they were trudging back to the lodge. "I don't care much for squirrels, but a fresh fish freshly fried suits me right down to the ground."

"Better say down to the bottom of your stomach, Jack," returned Gif, and at this the three boys had to laugh.

That night it looked as if it would storm again, the sky getting very dark and the wind rising rapidly.

"Gee, I hope the wind doesn't blow some of the trees down," cried Randy, as the wind increased in velocity, sending the leaves flying in all directions. "One might hit the building and knock it flat."

"Oh, don't be so cheerful!" cried Gif. "It's bad enough to hear that wind whistle without your trying to scare us to death."

The wind continued to blow strongly for several hours. There was, however, little rain, and presently, about midnight, the storm seemed to pass to the northward and all became quiet once more. Then the boys went to bed and soon all of them were sound asleep.

The next morning the others were glad to learn that Andy felt much better. He was, of course, still sore and somewhat stiff, but he managed to walk around fairly well and announced that he was willing to do whatever the others suggested.

"Well, I don't suggest hunting," said Spouter. "There is next to nothing to bring down at this season of the year. Of course we can go fishing again; but why not go over to the nearest end of the lake and have a good swim? We can laze around in the sun and have lots of fun."

This proposition met with instant approval, and the boys got ready to start out immediately after breakfast had been eaten and the lodge tidied up.

"I'll tell you what we can do," suggested Randy. "Why not have a swimming race? I don't mean a little two-cent affair, but a real race, say, across the lake and back."

"No such race for me," declared Andy. "You fellows can race and I'll be the judge and the stake holder. What are the stakes going to be? Why not make it a quart of ice-cream? Then while you're doing the swimming I'll place the ice-cream in a safe spot."

"Yes, where none of us will be able to get at it even if we win it," laughed Gif. "If there is any stake put up we'll have to make you give a bond so that we'll be sure the fellow who wins it gets it," and then there was a laugh.

The boys were about ready to start when Jack sat down to fix one of his shoes. As he was doing this Fred gave a sudden exclamation.

"Listen! Don't I hear somebody calling us?"

All listened, and presently from a distance they heard a cry.

"Hello, Jack Rover! Hello, Andy! Randy! Fred! Where are you?" and this cry was repeated several times.

"It's somebody after us!" cried Randy, and then yelled as loudly as he could:

"This way! This way for the Rovers! Hello there! Who are you?"

"I'm Pete Apgar!" came the distant reply. "Where are you?"

"We're up here at the hunting lodge!" called Jack. "This way, Pete!" and he continued to call until the person he was addressing came into view.

"Pete must have important news of some kind or else he wouldn't come up here this time of day," said Fred. "Why, he must have started from the farm last night!"

Pete Apgar was a young man who worked by the day in and around Dexter's Corners. Quite a little of his time was put in at Valley Brook Farm and he had already spoken for a steady place on the Stevenson estate when that should be ready for occupancy.

"Gosh all hemlock!" panted Pete Apgar, as he came up and sank down on a bench and began to fan himself with the straw hat he wore. "I thought I was never going to get here. Some hike, I'll say, from Valley Brook Farm to this place! I've been on the go ever since ten o'clock last night."

"What brought you?" asked Jack quickly. "No bad news, I hope?"

"I'm sorry to say it is bad news, Jack," was Apgar's reply.

"Somebody ill at the farm, or is it worse?" put in Randy.

"No, everybody's all right on the farm, although old Grandpop Rover ain't as good as he might be. But this news is from New York—from your folks down there. There's been a robbery."

"A robbery!" came simultaneously from all the young fellows.

"That's it," and Pete Apgar continued to fan himself. He was almost out of breath and gladly took a cup of water which Gif considerately got for him.

"What was robbed—our houses?" asked Fred.

"No, it wasn't your houses. It was down in your fathers' place of business in Wall Street. A big hold-up of some kind."

"A hold-up in the offices in Wall Street!" gasped Jack, and then he added quickly: "Was anybody shot?"

"I don't know none of the particulars," replied the farmhand. "A telegram came to your Uncle Randolph that the offices in Wall Street had been robbed and that he was to let you fellows know at once. So they sent me up here pellmell to tell you. I got a ride in Fenny's flivver as far as the bridge road. That was as far as he could take me, and I hoofed it the rest of the way. But I did stop at Bill Jandle's place early this morning and asked him to be in readiness with his flivver providing I could find you fellows and you wanted to ride home from there."

"I'm glad you did that, Pete," said Jack quickly. "It will save us a long tramp, and we can make time by riding even if we have to go away around by the bridge route instead of by the ford."

"You didn't get any more of the particulars about the robbery?" asked Andy.

"No. There wasn't any particulars. When I left the farm your Uncle Randolph was trying to get your folks on the long distance 'phone. But the storm the other day had knocked out some of the wires and they wasn't repaired yet; so he couldn't get anything. He said he would send Jack Ness down to the railroad station to try to get a message through by telegraph, but he was afraid the operator would be gone for the night, and in that case he'd not be able to do anything until this morning. Your uncle was all upset, and so was your aunt and your grandfather, not knowing how bad things might be."

"Well, they must be pretty bad, or otherwise our folks wouldn't send for us," said Jack.

"I guess you're right," added Randy. "For all we know, the Wall Street offices may have been cleaned out completely in this hold-up."

CHAPTER XIV
A DARING HOLD-UP

THE BOYS CONTINUED TO question Pete Apgar and at the same time packed up their belongings with all possible haste. Gif and Spouter assisted the Rover boys, knowing that their chums wanted to return to Valley Brook Farm as soon as it could be done.

"I hope this doesn't prove as bad as you think it," said Gif to Jack.

"So do I, Gif," was the reply. "But you know as well as I do that there have been a number of very daring hold-ups in the city during the past few years. Why, only a few months ago I read in the papers about a Maiden Lane jewelry firm being cleaned out of a hundred thousand dollars' worth of unset diamonds."

"I don't see how they could get a great deal at the offices," put in Andy. "I know they're very careful about the securities and keep most of the stuff in the safe or in the bank deposit boxes."

"Well, that's just it! Suppose they had a lot of stuff in the safe and the safe happened to be open when the hold-up men came in?"

"Oh, well, don't cross a bridge until you come to it, fellows," admonished Spouter. "Of course it may be bad enough, but not as bad as it might be. Perhaps by the time we get back to the farm your Uncle Randolph will have had some particulars by 'phone or telegraph."

In fifteen minutes the Rover boys and their chums were ready to start. The wooden shutters had been placed over the windows of the lodge and the door securely locked. Then the lads took up their rolls and other equipment.

"Andy, you had better let Pete carry your roll," said Jack. "You'll have trouble enough keeping up with us with that sore hip of yours."

"Sure, I'll carry his stuff," said the farmhand readily.

"Sorry to cut your outing up here short," said Jack to Gif and Spouter, as the party trudged along.

"Oh, don't say a word about that, Jack!" cried Spouter. "We expected to go back in a day or two, anyhow. Our only concern is this bad news. I hope the hold-up proves to be a small affair."

Hiking along in the direction of the Jandle farm, the boys could think of nothing but the news Pete Apgar had brought and indulged in all sorts of speculations concerning what had taken place.

When they came in sight of the Jandle farm they found Bill Jandle ready with his flivver, a dilapidated affair that looked as if it might fall apart at any moment. Near him stood his wife and his red-headed son.

"On hand, as I said I'd be," said the farmer to Apgar. And then he grinned at the boys as he added: "This will give me a chance to pay you back for shooting them pesky crows."

"Wisht I was going with you, Pop," said the red-headed boy wistfully.

"Got to put it off till another time, Tommy," returned his father. "We're going to have one mighty load as it is."

"If you can't carry all of us I'll walk," declared Gif. "Pete, here, can show me the way."

"Yes, and I'll walk too," put in Spouter.

"Oh, I guess this old bus will carry the lot. Only you'll have to hang on the best you can," said Bill Jandle.

The boys piled in, some sitting on the laps of others and the farmhand took a seat in an open doorway with his feet on the mudguard. Then, with a series of loud chuggings and a series of accompanying shivers, the flivver started away from the Jandle farm, Mrs. Jandle and Tommy waving a farewell.

It was a ride not easily forgotten. The way was unusually rough and more than once it looked as if every spring on the machine might be broken. The boys were pitched from one side of the car to the other and the farmhand had all he could do to keep from slipping off into the roadway.

"Ta—ta—talk about riding in a Pullman!" spluttered Andy. "Isn't this the smoothest ever?"

"Look out, Andy, or you'll bite off your tongue," warned Fred.

"Now hold on, all of you!" shouted Bill Jandle, and then they went down a long hill over the rough rocks in a fashion that all but upset the flivver and caused some of the occupants to wonder whether they would come out of the adventure alive.

At the foot of the hill they crossed the Swift River on a rickety bridge, every plank of which slapped and thumped as they passed over it. Then, however, they struck a much better road, and a short time later came in sight of the farm.

"We want to pay you for your services, Mr. Jandle," said Jack, as they turned into the lane. "What do you think it ought to be?"

"That's all right, Rover. You fellows did me a good turn when you shot those crows. Let us call it square."

"No, you let me pay you," returned Jack in a low voice, for he could easily see that Bill Jandle was rather pinched for money. And then he passed over a five-dollar bill which the farmer pocketed with great satisfaction.

Their coming had been noted, and the Rover boys were met on the veranda by their uncle and aunt and also their grandfather, all of whom were in a state of great mental excitement.

"I thought you'd never get here!" exclaimed their Uncle Randolph nervously. "This is an awful happening—truly awful!" and he wiped the perspiration from his brow.

"Just think of bandits holding up your fathers' offices!" burst out Aunt Martha. "Isn't it dreadful? I can't help but think that maybe somebody was shot!"

"I wish I had been down there with a pistol!" quavered Grandfather Rover, his head bobbing from side to side. "I'd just like to get a shot at such rascals!" and he shook his cane as if to knock out some bandit right then and there.

"Have you received any more news?" asked Randy quickly.

"Nothing since we got that first message," said Uncle Randolph. "We've been trying to use the 'phone, but wires are out of commission somewhere along the line. We thought we had New York once, but it was only Binghamton."

"We ought to be able to get into communication by telegraph," said Jack.

"Jack Ness went down to the station an hour ago. I gave him a message to send and he was to wait for a reply."

"Let's go down to the station too," put in Fred quickly. "There is no use of hanging around here if the telephone is out of order."

"I think I'll stay here. Maybe the telephone will come in before a great while," said Andy. The soreness in his hip had not been improved by the rough ride in Bill Jandle's flivver.

Gif and Spouter elected to remain with Andy and then Jack, Randy and Fred ran off to the garage and brought out one of the touring cars, and in another moment the three were on their way to the railroad station at Oak Run, across the river from Dexter's Corners.

"Perhaps we'll meet Jack Ness coming back," said Fred. "If we do, stop him, by all means."

However, they did not meet the hired man. But on the outskirts of Dexter's Corners they passed an elegant sport car under the wheel of which rode Joe Sedley, smoking a cigarette and with his cap pulled well down over his eyes. Sedley simply glared at the Rovers, refusing to return their nods of recognition.

"Gee, he must still be sore over the way the horse race was decided," was Fred's comment.

"Well, Jack won that race, and that's all there is to it," put in Randy loyally.

"He'll never admit it," said the oldest Rover. And then he became silent and for the first time since Pete Apgar had brought the news of the hold-up Jack's thoughts reverted to Ruth and he wondered if the girl had sent him a letter or if she had corresponded in any way with Sedley. In the excitement of the occasion none of the Rovers who had dashed off to the railroad station had thought to ask at the farmhouse if any letters had come in.

They sped through the village and across the Swift River and then up to the railroad station at Oak Run. Here they saw another one of the farm turnouts and then ran across Jack Ness, who held up a telegram.

"It's for your uncle," said the hired man, "but I guess you'd better open it and read it."

"I will," said Jack, and did so. The telegram ran as follows:

Impossible to get telephone service. Hold-up at offices bad. Want some particulars from boys. Send them home at once.

Richard Rover

While reading this telegram the boys heard the whistle of a locomotive and presently the local train from the Junction rolled into the station and several passengers alighted while others got aboard. A trunk was taken off and several bundles of newspapers followed.

"Here come the New York papers!" cried Fred. "Come on—let's get some of them! They may have some particulars of the hold-up."

Two of the bundles of papers were for one of the Oak Run storekeepers, and a clerk was on hand to receive them. Quickly the bundles were torn open and each of the lads possessed himself of a metropolitan newspaper.

"Here it is!" cried Randy, scanning the front page rapidly, and he showed the following:

DARING HOLD-UP IN WALL STREET OFFICES OF THE ROVER COMPANY LOOTED

Five Daring Bandits Hold Up Four Clerks Just Before Closing Time and Make Off with Securities Worth $100,000.

Police Search in Vain for Clues. None of the Officers of the
Company Present when the Hold-Up Occurred.

There followed a somewhat mixed-up account of how the hold-up had
occurred and what the Rovers had to say concerning it.

"Well, this certainly is news!" declared Jack, after reading not only this
account but also those which the other newspapers presented.

"But what do you suppose this telegram means?" asked Randy anxiously.
"What do they want us to give information about?"

"That remains to be seen," said Fred. And then, all of a sudden, he gave a
low whistle. "I guess this means good-bye to Captain Corning's hunt for the
Margarita," he added.

"The only thing we can do is to get down to New York as soon as possible,"
declared Jack. "Gee, I wish I was down there now! I'll bet there's plenty of
excitement."

"If only they catch those bandits and get back the stuff they took!" murmured Fred. "A hundred thousand dollars! Just think of it!"

"This is the first newspaper account, Fred," said Jack. "It was probably
written in a great hurry. You must remember this paper was printed some
time last evening. There may be a lot of other news since then."

The boys knew they could get a train for the Junction in two hours. This
would connect with the New York Express and would bring them home late
in the afternoon.

"We'll get back to the farm and make it somehow," declared Jack. "Come
on!" and away they went, back to Valley Brook Farm, as fast as they could,
with Jack Ness following.

As might be expected, the telegram and the articles in the newspapers
concerning the hold-up created more excitement than ever at the farm. As
old as he was, Grandfather Rover wanted to go down to New York, and it took
quite some talk on the part of Jack and Aunt Martha to make him change his
mind. Uncle Randolph, however, insisted upon accompanying the boys.

"You'll have to excuse us, fellows," said Jack to Gif and Spouter.

"Oh, that's all right, Jack. Go ahead. We'll be all right," said Gif quickly.

"We were leaving in a day or two, anyhow," said Spouter.

"They're to stay over to-night," said Aunt Martha. "I'd rather have them
here with your Uncle Randolph gone," she added; and so it was arranged.

Only a few letters from their boy chums had come in for the Rovers during
their outing. There was no word from Ruth, and this gave Jack a momentary
pang, although he did not allow the others to know it.

It did not take the lads or their Uncle Randolph long to pack. Then the boys said good-bye to their chums and to the others, and in a few minutes more were on their way to the railroad station. Their uncle and Jack Ness accompanied them.

"Good-bye and good luck!" shouted Gif.

"Take care of yourselves!" added Spouter.

"We'll try to," said Jack. "Hope you both have a fine time on the rest of your outing."

"And we hope your folks get back all the stuff that was stolen," cried Gif, as the auto moved away.

CHAPTER XV
HOW THE ROVER COMPANY WAS HELD UP

IF THE ROVER BOYS were worked up over the hold-up in Wall Street, their excitement was as nothing compared to that of their parents.

"I must confess I'm completely stumped."

It was Sam Rover who spoke. The three brothers were closeted in an inner office of the company and Fred's father stood by a window gazing blankly at nothing in particular.

"What gets me is the skillful manner in which this hold-up was planned," came from Tom Rover. "That telegram calling me to Philadelphia was a fake, just as the telegram that took Sam to Boston to see the head of the Eighteenth National Bank was a cooked-up affair."

"Yes, and see how they got me out of the way," said Dick Rover dismally. "When that fellow—whoever he was—telephoned to me that there had been an accident in the subway uptown and that Dora had been hurt, what was there for me to do but to rush out, jump into the subway and get uptown just as quickly as possible? Why, it took me nearly an hour to locate Dora because she wasn't at home, and then I found out that she had received a fake message from Mrs. Watson asking her to come over at once in regard to some church matters."

"The whole thing was certainly well thought out," went on the father of the twins. "It's a wonder they didn't send everybody in the office off on a wild-goose chase," and Tom smiled grimly.

"I've been trying to think who might have done this," continued Dick slowly, tapping his desk with a pencil as he spoke. "Of course, the police detectives think it was done by one of the well-organized bands of hold-up men in and around New York. But just the same, we know that we have a certain number of personal enemies who wouldn't like anything better than to pull off such a job as this."

"Who among our enemies would have the nerve to do it?" asked Sam Rover. "Davenport and his gang are in jail, so they are eliminated. Now then, we know that old Josiah Crabtree is at liberty; but I don't think he'd have the nerve to attempt anything of this sort."

"He might not have the nerve to play the part of a bandit at the offices, but he might help the real criminals by, for instance, doing some of that telephoning or telegraphing.

"Of course, there are a lot of other fellows who'd be only too glad to make trouble for us," went on Tom, after a pause. "First of all, there is Nelson Martell who used to be in business down here and who lost out in the oil fields, and along with him is that chap Slogwell Brown, and then their two sons, Slugger and Nappy, who have had so much trouble with our boys."

"And, yes—don't forget some of the other fellows, like Mr. Werner and his good-for-nothing son Gabe."

"Oh, there are plenty of those fellows who would be glad to take the very shirts from our backs!" cried Sam. "Some of the fellows who tried to injure us at Putnam Hall and at Brill College—fellows like Jerry Koswell and his cronies."

There was a moment of silence between the three men, each evidently trying to do some hard thinking. Then Dick Rover motioned for his brothers to come closer.

"What do you think of that clerk of ours—Ken Greene?" he whispered, thus making certain that his voice would not carry to any of the outer offices of the company of which he was president.

"I don't like him, and never did," said Tom bluntly.

"Well, if he's perfectly honest, then he's a doughhead, and we certainly don't want him in these offices any longer," came from Sam. "Any fellow who will neglect his duties as Greene did deserves to be kicked out."

"Well, I intend to kick him out, but I won't do it just yet," said Jack's father. "We may want his testimony, and the detectives may want to question him further."

The senior Rovers had passed a hectic evening and an even more hectic night. None of them had been to bed, neither did any of them have the least desire to go to sleep. The nerves of each were at a high tension, and with good reason.

"If it was only our own stuff I wouldn't say so much," said Dick, with something like a groan. "But to have our best friends suffer too—well, it's something I can hardly stand."

"I don't believe Songbird Powell or Fred Garrison will blame us," returned Tom. "But what Mr. Stevenson will do is another matter. I'm afraid it may rough up matters between Jack and Ruth, Dick," and he gazed at his older brother questioningly.

"Well, if Mr. Stevenson gets sore I suppose we'll have to bear it," said Jack's father. "It's too bad, but I don't see what can be done. We're in a big hole, and that's all there is to it."

"No, it isn't!" cried Sam, just as sturdy and defiant in his manner as he had ever been. "We're in a hole, that's true. But it's our business to climb out of it, and we're going to do it!"

"Let's hope we do so," returned Tom. "But it seems to me that hole is a good deal like a deep well and that we're just about as well off as a trio of frogs at the bottom thereof," and a flash of Tom's old-time humor asserted itself.

"Well, this talk doesn't seem to be getting us anywhere," said Dick, rising to his feet. "We'd better check up on those securities of which we were not certain and find out what steps can be taken so that no one will negotiate them."

The bare details of the hold-up were simple enough. The affair had occurred a few minutes before the regular time for closing the offices. As said before, Tom and Sam had been called out of town by fake telegrams and Dick had been called away by a telephone message which stated that his wife Dora had been hurt in a subway accident uptown. At the time of the hold-up one clerk and a messenger boy had been away from the offices on business, and as this was the dull season of the year a number of the others were away on their vacations. This left but a head bookkeeper and three clerks in charge when the bandits had entered quietly, closing and locking the door behind them.

The bandits had worn handkerchiefs tied across the lower parts of their faces and had had caps well drawn down over their foreheads. Each had been armed and, afraid of being shot, the head bookkeeper and the three clerks had submitted with scarcely a protest. They had been driven into a closet used for the storage of records and there they had been told to make a noise at the risk of their lives, and then the door had been locked upon them.

Having disposed of the help, the bandits had lost no time in looting the unlocked safe and also going through all the desks, breaking open those which were locked. They had worked quickly but effectively and had carried off everything of value.

As yet the total loss was problematic for the reason that it was not known how many of the securities which had been stolen were negotiable. Roughly speaking, the Rovers estimated that the loss would not be less than one hundred thousand dollars and might go to almost twice that amount.

The head bookkeeper was a middle-aged man named Frank Mason, and he had been with The Rover Company since its beginning. Mason was a good deal of a plodder, but all of the Rovers felt that he was thoroughly honest and could not have been connected in any way with the hold-up.

"It came like a thunder clap, Mr. Rover! Just like a thunder clap!" exclaimed Frank Mason in a wavering voice when asked. "I was never more surprised in my life than when I looked up and saw that man with a handkerchief tied over his face and with a pistol pointed right at my head."

"Have you any idea who the man was—or, in fact, who any of the men were?" Dick asked.

"Not the slightest, sir. I'm quite certain they were all strangers to me."

Mason's story was largely the story told by the other clerks. One of the young fellows, named Bronson, and another named Greene, had tried to make the Rovers and the police detectives believe that they had wanted to resist. But they had done nothing and the detectives were of the opinion that they had submitted meekly and were now drawing on their imaginations in the hope of getting their names in the limelight.

Half a dozen clues were being followed up, but so far without results. Several strangers who had been seen in and around the building before and after the hold-up were asked by the authorities, and one of the men was taken to police headquarters and kept over night. But nothing could be proved against this individual except that he was a good-for-nothing rounder, and he was allowed to go with the admonition to get out of the city as quickly as possible.

The most active men in the affair were the reporters, and Dick, Tom and Sam had all they could do to keep out of the clutches of the news gatherers, who wished to get every slightest detail of the hold-up. As we know, the morning papers had made a spread of the story, and the afternoon journals followed.

"Well, we're certainly getting a lot of notoriety," said Dick, when he and his brothers were on their way that evening to their homes on Riverside Drive. "But it's the kind of advertising I don't like."

"I'm afraid this hold-up is going to give The Rover Company a black eye," muttered Tom. "Some folks will think we're mighty careless in handling our securities and consequently they won't want to do business with us. However, hold-ups are real fashionable just now, so we're right in the swim," he added, with a queer sort of grin.

When the three men arrived at home they found that the boys had just come in. The lads had telephoned from the Grand Central Terminal to the offices and then, finding that their fathers had left, had come directly in a taxicab to Riverside Drive.

"No news, Jack," said Dick, in reply to a question from his son. "We're at a standstill, and so are the authorities. Our securities are gone and they and the bandits who took them have vanished into thin air."

"Do you mean to say no one saw them leave the offices or no one raised an alarm?" asked Randy.

"No one saw them leaving the building—or at least if they were seen, nobody paid any attention to them," replied Tom Rover. "But that isn't to be wondered at because our building has dozens of people coming and going all the time and there are any number of automobiles and taxicabs in the street."

"Well, what of the fellows who were locked in the closet?" demanded Fred.

"They remained in the closet until everything became quiet in the offices. Then they knocked on the door for a minute or two, and as none of the bandits came to make them keep quiet they at last forced the door open. Then Mason ran for the telephone and notified the police while the other clerks ran out in the corridor and went down in an elevator to the street to see if they could catch sight of the rascals. But that must have been at least five to ten minutes after the bandits had taken their leave."

"And how much of a loss will it be, Dad?" asked Jack, with increasing interest.

"So far as I have been able to figure up, there will be a positive loss on bonds of a little over one hundred thousand dollars," said his parent. "Then a number of other securities are missing, and how many of these can be negotiated is a question. The loss might possibly come up to nearly two hundred thousand dollars."

"Yes, but listen, Uncle Dick!" broke in Randy. "I know you carry insurance on all your stuff. Wasn't this covered?"

"That's the hardest part of the story," said Dick Rover, his face twitching slightly as he spoke. "We've been carrying insurance on all the stuff, but the insurance ran out less than a week ago and the clerk who had charge of this, a fellow named Ken Greene, failed to have the insurance renewed. As a consequence the entire loss falls on our own shoulders."

CHAPTER XVI
A GLOOMY OUTLOOK

"No insurance!" cried Fred, in dismay.

"Gee, that certainly is the worst news yet!" came from Andy.

"What's the reason Greene didn't have the insurance renewed?" demanded Jack. "Didn't he know it had run out?"

"Yes, he admits that he knew it and that he had taken the matter up with several insurance companies a week before this insurance ran out. He says he thought he could get better rates for us and was going to submit the new rates to me. But then, he claims, a lot of extra outside work was piled on him, and in the rush of that the insurance slipped his mind."

"Dick, I think that's a fishy yarn!" exclaimed Sam Rover. "You know how all those insurance companies are—hungry for business. If Greene had gone after them as he says he did, they would have pestered the life out of us to have their particular line of insurance accepted."

"Well, I'm inclined to agree with you, and, as I said before, I'm going to fire Greene a little later on. But no matter what we can prove against the young idiot, the fact remains that we have no insurance and therefore if the securities are not recovered the loss will fall entirely on us."

"What about the money Mr. Stevenson and Gif's father and Spouter's father put in?" asked Jack.

"As they are now stockholders in the company, the loss will fall on their shoulders as well as ours," said his father.

"Did Spouter's father put up the extra money that was coming from him?" queried Randy.

"He did—the day before the hold-up. He brought in some first-class railroad bonds, and they were among the bonds that were stolen. They had been placed in the office safe because we wanted to list them properly and take down the numbers, and then we were going to offer them to one of the bond houses because we needed the cash."

"Needed the cash!" broke in Fred quickly. "In that case I suppose this loss is going to hit the company pretty hard?" and he looked at his father as he spoke.

"Yes, Fred, we might as well let you boys know the truth," said Sam Rover. "Just at the present time we are under heavy obligations to three banks here in New York, and that was one reason why we took in this additional capital from our old friends and Mr. Stevenson. As you know, we have been branching out, not only with our business here in Wall Street, but also with our mines in the West and our oil well holdings in the South, and all of those things cramped us a little for cash."

"If the money isn't recovered, what then?" asked Randy bluntly.

"We won't talk about that just yet," said Dick Rover, but his tone showed that he was much disturbed.

"Of course you have notified Mr. Stevenson and the others?" said Jack.

"Oh, yes. We notified all our stockholders by 'phone or telegraph," said Tom Rover. "We're going to hold a special meeting to-morrow morning at ten o'clock and then decide on what is best to be done."

"Well, as far as I'm concerned, Uncle Tom, you can have every cent I have in the bank," declared Jack promptly.

"And you can have what I've got, too," came simultaneously from Fred and the twins.

"It's nice for you to say that, boys," said the twins' father. "How much could you rake and scrape together if you had to?"

The boys made a hasty calculation, counting in the money they had received in the oil fields and when they and Ira Small had uncovered the pirates' treasure, and Jack announced the result.

"We've got twenty-eight thousand dollars," he said, a bit proudly. "That isn't half bad, is it?"

"It's very good," said his father. "I'm glad to know you boys are saving your money and not spending it recklessly as so many young fellows do. But I'm afraid, Jack, that that amount would only be a drop in the bucket."

"How much do you need, Dad, if it's any of my business?"

"We'll need a hundred thousand dollars inside of the next two weeks and two hundred thousand dollars a month later."

"We could have taken care of our finances very nicely if this hold-up had not occurred," said Tom Rover. "You see, we have other securities and on those we could raise a loan. But now we may have to sacrifice those, and that will entail a heavy loss because I'm sure the securities are going up in value and ought to be kept."

"Dad, you said in your telegram that you wanted to question us," broke in Jack. "What was it you wanted to know?"

"We've been thinking that it is possible this hold-up was engineered by some of our old enemies who may be in cahoots with some real bandits. We were thinking that possibly you might know of something that would throw light on the subject."

"We have seen Slugger Brown and Nappy Martell in an automobile in the vicinity of Valley Brook Farm and one night the girls declared they saw Slugger Brown looking in at one of the windows."

"Is that so! That sounds interesting."

"I can see how that might fit in," came from Sam Rover.

"How could that fit in with a hold-up down here?" asked Andy, in wonder.

"In this way," said the twins' father. "Your uncles and I all received fake messages taking us away from the offices when the hold-up occurred. Your Aunt Dora also received a fake message taking her away from home. That looks to me as if it was planned to keep as many of us away from the offices as possible. That being so, perhaps Slugger Brown and Nappy Martell were hired by some others—maybe their own fathers—to watch you fellows and report if you intended to come back here. It's just possible that they may have had orders to try to detain you if you started for New York. They must know that when you're in the city you're frequent visitors at the offices and would raise an alarm at once if you happened to get down there and found the place locked up during business hours or got there just before the hold-up took place."

"There might be something in that," said Jack slowly. Thereupon the boys gave a few particulars concerning the appearance of their enemies in the vicinity of the farm and then asked for more particulars concerning the hold-up.

The talk did not come to an end until dinner was announced. Then the various families separated, agreeing to come together again in Tom's library after the repast was over.

"Oh, Jack, isn't it a terrible happening?" said his mother, as she took him in her arms. There were tears in Dora's eyes as she spoke. Her face was pale and haggard and showed plainly the loss of sleep.

"Oh, Mother, you mustn't take it so hard," he returned, kissing her. "I'm sure it will come out all right in the end. They'll catch those bandits and get most of the securities back, I'm sure of it!"

"Well, I certainly hope so." But Mrs. Rover shook her head sadly as she spoke.

Dinner in all the three connecting houses that evening was a sombre affair. Fred's mother was even more dejected than Dora Rover, and the twins could do little to cheer up Nellie.

"Why, boys, don't you understand?" said Tom's wife. "This may bankrupt The Rover Company!"

"Oh, come, come, Nellie! Not quite as bad as all that," said Tom. Yet, in spite of his attempt at light-heartedness, the twins saw that their father was far more worried than he was willing to admit.

Randolph Rover had spent most of the time with the mothers of the boys, quieting them as best he could. In coming down to the city the old gentleman who had made scientific farming his hobby had been busy doing a lot of figuring, and now, when the dinner in Dick Rover's mansion came to a close, he called his nephew to one side.

"I've been figuring on those securities I possess which aren't deposited with The Rover Company," he announced. "Outside of the farm, I've got about eighteen thousand dollars. If it will do you any good, Dick, you can have it, and if it's necessary I'll sell the farm too. That ought to be worth at least twenty-five thousand dollars, the way values are going up in that vicinity."

"That's awfully good of you, Uncle Randolph," said Dick, and in spite of himself his voice choked with emotion. "But I'm hoping we can get our securities back or make the necessary arrangements with the banks to tide us over. But you're awfully good, and I'll never forget it," and he wrung his uncle's hand heartily.

"Your father wanted to come. He wanted to go after those bandits himself," continued the uncle. "We had quite a time to make him change his plans and remain on the farm." It may be added here that Anderson Rover was considerably older than his brother Randolph and far from as vigorous in health.

Left to himself, Jack walked slowly up to his own room where his bag had been placed by one of the servants. The former major of the Colby Hall battalion had never been in a more serious mood than at present.

He realized that the hold-up in Wall Street might be fraught with dire results. If the securities were not recovered The Rover Company might go bankrupt and the fortunes that it had taken years to accumulate might be completely swept away.

"Dad and the rest of us would have to start all over again," he told himself. "I'm young, and it wouldn't be such a hard thing for me to do, but it would certainly be rough on dad and Uncle Sam and Uncle Tom, not to say anything about mother and Aunt Nellie and Aunt Grace and the girls."

Then Jack's thoughts drifted to the Stevensons and he walked over to the chiffonier upon which, in a pretty silver frame, rested a photograph of Ruth, a smiling, tantalizing picture that made Jack's heart jump every time he gazed at it. What effect would this loss have upon Mr. Stevenson and his daughter? Would Ruth's father blame the officers of The Rover Company for neglect in not looking after the insurance and in not safeguarding the offices better?

What would Ruth have to say when he saw her or when she wrote to him, provided she did write?

"Maybe she won't write at all," he thought dolefully. "Her father may be as mad as a hornet and she may take his part. And then, if we lose all our money, what right will I have to ask her to wait for me when there is such a rich chap as Joe Sedley hanging around? I'm sure he'd marry her in a minute if he could get her," and then Jack heaved a long sigh that came from the very bottom of his heart.

CHAPTER XVII
REAL FRIENDS

THE CONFERENCE IN TOM ROVER's library lasted until well past midnight. There were present not only the Rovers, but a number of other business men, and all sorts of plans for continuing business at the offices in Wall Street were thrashed out.

Several of the outsiders were liberal with their advice, but when it came to real assistance Dick Rover and his brothers quickly realized that they would have to depend almost entirely on themselves for whatever was done.

The boys were not wanted at this conference, and so withdrew to the library in Jack's home. Here the four held a discussion fully as animated as that going on next door.

"Dad admits that things look mighty black," said Randy. "But he cautioned Andy and myself not to say too much before mother, because she's worried to death as it is."

"And that's just what dad told me to be careful of," put in Fred. "I never saw my mother look worse! Why, you'd think somebody in the family had died!"

"Well, we've got to admit that it is serious—the most serious thing that ever happened to us as far as our fortunes are concerned," returned Jack. "This hold-up may wipe out The Rover Company entirely. The company has obligations totaling three hundred thousand dollars and all of these have got to be met inside of six weeks. Of course, they may get an extension of time from the banks and their other creditors. But unless the missing securities are recovered it isn't likely that those extensions will be for long."

"But their credit ought to be good; the company has always stood A, Number One!" cried Andy.

"Yes. And that will help some, so dad says. But it won't help enough," said Jack. "I really don't know what they can do unless they can get some of their friends to come to the front and help them out, and I know dad and your fathers would hate to ask them to do that under present circumstances, when everything looks so black."

"What about the girls? Are they going to stay with Ruth now that this thing has happened?" asked Randy.

"Mother telegraphed to Mary that she had better come home," said Fred. "I suppose Martha will come with her. More than likely they'll be just as anxious as we were to know what's going on."

"I wonder if Slugger Brown and Nappy Martell are really implicated in this?" mused Jack. "If they are, then the thing for us to do would be to try to locate them and force them to tell the truth."

"If they were implicated, you can make sure that now the hold-up has been pulled off they'll keep out of sight," said Randy. "The fellows who did that may be thousands of miles away by this time."

"And to think the police haven't been able to round up anybody!" sighed Andy.

"Well, it's not so easy to trace a criminal as some people think," returned his twin. "Sometimes they catch a crook more by good luck than by cleverness."

"Well, then, let's hope that we have luck in landing these bandits," came from Fred. "Wish I could get my hands on 'em!"

The next day was a busy one for the older Rovers. A conference was held at the offices in Wall Street, and this was attended by the fathers of the boys, as well as by Songbird Powell, Fred Garrison, and several other men. Somewhat to the Rovers' surprise, Mr. Stevenson was not present.

"Mr. Stevenson hasn't said any of our telegrams," said Dick to his brothers, just as the conference got under way. "Perhaps he's away from home and hasn't even heard of the hold-up." And this surmise proved to be correct.

The outsiders at the meeting wanted to know if the authorities had as yet reported anything of importance and were much disappointed when Dick stated that so far as he and his brothers knew no real information concerning the hold-up men had yet been brought to light.

"The authorities have a number of hold-up men under suspicion," said he. "And all of these are being watched by the detectives. One of the older detectives thinks this job may have been engineered by two fellows known as Lefty Ditini, so called because he's left-handed, and Black Ronombo, two fellows who are supposed to be West Indians or, possibly, Mexicans. They're also looking for three slick bandits who have been operating in Philadelphia and Buffalo, because they handle jobs in exactly the same way this affair was handled."

Dick then went on making a little speech and recited such particulars of the affair as he could and ended by telling of the securities that were missing and of the fact that the insurance on the documents had run out, owing to the neglect of one of their clerks.

"I presume we are responsible for not keeping track of the insurance," he continued. "We should have watched that matter more closely."

"Well, we're all liable to make mistakes," put in Gif Garrison's father quickly. "Of course, it's a great shock, Dick. But I want to say right now that I'm not going to blame either you or Tom or Sam for what has happened."

"And neither am I going to blame you," put in Songbird Powell. "Why, this hold-up might have happened to any of us. Wasn't my house robbed last summer? While we were at dinner in the dining room the thieves crawled up on a second story porch and went through all the upper rooms, taking money and jewelry to the tune of over two thousand dollars. And we've never heard of what was stolen to this day."

"Yes, I remember that," said Tom.

"It's good of you to stand by us," said Dick, looking gratefully at his former school chums. "But now let us come to business and see just what can be done toward getting the Company out of this mess."

The conference lasted until the middle of the afternoon and all sorts of ways and means were discussed to bridge over the difficulty. Fred Garrison came forward with an additional twenty thousand dollars and Songbird Powell offered another fifteen thousand dollars, and these two sums were tentatively accepted by Dick and his brothers.

In the midst of the talk four telegrams were received, two from their old school chums, George Granbury and Hans Mueller and the others from Stanley Browne and Spud Jackson who had been with them at Brill College. All of these men tendered their sincerest sympathy and each said he would help out if an endorsement of notes was needed.

"Well, that shows we've certainly got some friends!" said Sam, and his eyes grew misty as he read one telegram after another. "Good for George, Hans, Spud and Stanley!"

By a hard effort and a good deal of close figuring on the part of all of the older Rovers the Company managed to fix things so that the obligations amounting to about one hundred thousand dollars and falling due within the next two weeks would be met. But what could be done about the two hundred thousand coming due a month later was still a question.

"We'll have to see some of the bank officials about that," said Tom. "They ought to be able to tide us over, especially if we can get the right kind of endorsements for our notes." Yet even as he spoke he knew that the prospects were not encouraging, for the money market was just then very tight.

The boys visited the offices and took a look around the premises. All of the clerks were once again at work and Jack and his cousins gazed at Ken Greene in anything but a friendly manner.

"If it hadn't been for that puddin'head the Company would be all right," whispered Fred to the others. "Just think of one clerk like that being able to put a company like this in the hole just because he forgot to do his duty!"

"It's like the soldier who goes to sleep when he's on guard," put in Andy. "For two pins I'd like to give him the thrashing of his life!"

"Well, as for that, I guess we'd all like to do it," came from Jack.

When the boys returned to Riverside Drive they found that Martha and Mary had just arrived. The girls were excited and tried to ask a dozen questions at once.

"Mrs. Stevenson was just as upset as anybody," said Martha in reply to a question from her brother. "Mr. Stevenson was away on a fishing trip and she didn't know how to get hold of him. And what do you think, Jack? Half of the money that Ruth's father put into The Rover Company belonged to Mrs. Stevenson! So she'll stand to lose just as much as her husband."

"And what did Ruth have to say about the affair?"

"Oh, she didn't know what to say. It took them both so much by surprise that they were almost stunned. Then Mrs. Stevenson went into hysterics when she thought all that money might be lost, and Ruth had all she could do to quiet her."

"Did Ruth blame dad for what happened?"

"She did and she didn't. She thought it was awfully queer that none of the officers of the company was at the offices when the hold-up happened and she also thought it was queer that they should have had so many securities on hand. She thought such valuable things were either kept locked in the safe or else locked in the bank vaults."

"Well, dad would have been there, only he got the fake 'phone call that mother had been hurt in a subway accident. And as for having the securities on hand, there is a good explanation about that, although I'm afraid I can't just explain it to you. Some of these securities were being listed to be sold. They all had to be inspected, and that was the reason they were at the offices and not in the bank vaults. Of course, the majority of them were in the office safe, but that was open because it is usually kept open during office hours. Dad says, however, that they should have been locked in an inner compartment, although he supposes the bandits could easily have opened such a compartment with the tools they probably carried."

"Well, it's too bad. Mrs. Stevenson cried quite a good deal and once she let out that she expected to give Ruth five thousand dollars' worth of the securities when Ruth became of age and another five thousand on her wedding day, if she ever got married."

"Well, it's too bad, Martha, and nobody feels it any more than I do," said Jack, and turned away, his lips quivering.

Instantly his sister was at his side and had her arm over his shoulder.

"Jack dear, don't think that I don't understand," she whispered. "I do! And I feel it just as much as you do! But don't think too hard of Ruth. She has been all upset by the way her mother takes it and by the fact that her father could not be found. I'm sure when she calms down she will understand it better."

"Maybe," Jack said. "But just now it looks as if everything was crumbling under our feet."

A surprise awaited the Rovers just as the men of the family came home from Wall Street. They had just stepped into the house when a tall gentleman leaped from a taxicab and ran up the steps after Dick.

"Larry Colby!" exclaimed Jack's father, greeting the head of Colby Hall with a hearty handclasp. "I'm glad to see you!"

"I thought I'd catch you here rather than at the offices," said the master of Colby Hall. "I started for New York just as soon as I heard of your trouble."

Colonel Colby was greeted warmly by not only the older Rovers, but also the lads who had attended his school so many years. The colonel did not waste words, but went immediately to the subject nearest to his heart.

"I knew you might be wanting assistance," he said, "and I thought I'd come here and tell you that I stand ready to do what I can. I haven't got any great amount of cash I can put up—most of my money goes into improvements at the school—but what I have you are welcome to. And if my name counts for anything, you are welcome to use that too."

For the moment Dick could hardly speak, he was so overcome by his emotion. Then he blurted out his thanks, remarking at the same time that he had heard the same words not only from Fred Garrison and Songbird Powell, but also from Spud Jackson, Stanley Browne, George Granbury and Hans Mueller. "I'll tell you what—old friends are best!" he said. "Every one of them is sticking to us like glue!"

CHAPTER XVIII
FOLLOWING KEN GREENE

TWO DAYS SLIPPED BY and the authorities continued to do what they could about the hold-up, but without making material progress. In the meantime The Rover Company had called in the services of a private detective agency and the men of this concern also went over the ground carefully, trying to gain some clue which might enable them to run down the evildoers.

All of the clerks in the offices were asked over and over again, and presently Ken Greene was given such a grilling that he grew angry and announced in a loud voice that he would give up his job.

"I didn't do anything wrong and I'm not going to be made the goat in this affair," grumbled Greene, a tall, sallow-faced lad with rather shifty eyes. "Getting that insurance renewed was the business of the officers of this company. All you are paying me here is thirty dollars a week salary, and I can get that anywhere, and more too! I'm through!"

"You have simply saved yourself, Greene, from being discharged," said Dick cheerfully. "I was going to fire you Saturday, anyway. You can go at once. And don't expect any recommendations."

"I'm not asking for them," was the quick retort, and then, having received his wages, Ken Greene put on his hat and coat and left the offices, banging the door after him.

"I think that fellow ought to be followed and watched," declared Tom to his brothers, when he saw Greene getting ready to leave.

"Say the word, Dad, and I'll follow him," put in Randy quickly. He and his brother were down at the offices at the time.

"All right, go ahead and do it. Only see that you don't get into any trouble. If Greene does anything that looks suspicious, telephone here or to the police."

The twins crowded into the elevator with Greene, who looked at them rather suspiciously. However, when the street floor was gained the clerk pushed his way out in a crowd of people and then Andy and Randy, though watching him, managed to keep out of the fellow's sight. Greene walked up to Broadway and there boarded a street car, getting off at Eighth Street and walking westward. Presently they saw him enter one of a long row of houses.

It was a boarding establishment kept by a Mrs. Dorsey, as they could see by a sign over the doorbell.

"Now the question is, is he going to stay at home awhile or will he be coming out soon?" remarked Randy.

"That remains to be seen," said his twin. "We might as well take it easy," and, obtaining a pint of freshly-roasted peanuts from a stand at the corner, the boys stationed themselves in a convenient doorway and started to watch.

In less than half an hour their vigilance was rewarded by seeing Ken Greene come forth from the boarding house. He had changed his suit and hat and now carried a tan suitcase in his hand.

"He's bound for somewhere!" exclaimed Andy. "Come on quick—don't let him slip us in the crowd."

Taking more care than ever that Greene should not see them, they followed the ex-clerk as he walked eastward crosstown until he reached the subway at Astor Place. Here he boarded a train going uptown, and they followed, keeping half a length of a crowded car between them and the man they were shadowing.

"Got any money with you, Randy?" asked his twin, as the train rolled uptown. "I've got the whole of forty cents with me."

"I've got eighty-five cents. I didn't expect to use anything more than my car fare when I went downtown."

"Then if this fellow rides very far or does any other sort or traveling, we'll be stumped."

In a very few minutes the train reached Forty-second Street, and here Ken Greene alighted and rushed over to one of the ticket windows in the Grand Central Terminal. Here he stopped for several minutes and then moved over to another window where Pullman accommodations were to be had.

"Excuse me!" exclaimed Randy, pushing his way up to the first window directly Greene had gone. "Did my friend who was just here get his ticket all right enough?" he asked the clerk while the lady who had expected to be waited on glared at him in anger.

"Who do you mean? The fellow who just got the ticket for the South?" asked the clerk pleasantly.

"I want to know if he got his ticket all the way through. I want to get mine just like it," stated Randy.

"You'll have to take your turn in line."

"Sure! And I beg your pardon," went on the Rover boy, bowing to the lady in question politely. "Only I wanted to make sure how far that ticket went. I don't want to go one way and have him go another. He slipped me in the crowd."

"He got a ticket to Galveston by the way of St. Louis."

"Oh, that's what I wanted to know! Thank you very much," and Randy slipped out of the crowd and rejoined his brother.

Ken Greene was already leaving the Pullman window, and now the twins saw him turning toward one of the gates leading to the train shed.

"He bought a ticket for Galveston, Texas," whispered Randy excitedly. "What do you think we ought to do?"

"We might have him held, but I think the best thing we can do is to let him go on. If he's in this plot and going to Galveston, he's doing it for a purpose. Let's make sure he gets on the train and find out if we can just what Pullman car he takes and what the number of the train is. Then, if the police want to do anything, they can have him arrested on the way."

They watched Ken Greene go through the gate and then Randy persuaded the gateman to allow him to pass without a ticket, stating that it was a matter of great importance concerning a fellow who had just gone on ahead. Then Randy, still keeping out of sight, saw Greene enter car No. 4 and take a seat by one of the windows. A few minutes later the train rumbled away out of the station.

"Well, that's that!" said Randy, as he rejoined his brother. "We've got the number of the train and the number of the car and I know he's seated on the left-hand side about the center, so the authorities can locate him almost anywhere along the line."

"Now that he's gone, might it not pay to go back to the boarding house and see if we can learn something more about him?" suggested Andy. "His boarding mistress might tell us something that would be valuable."

It did not take the twins long to return to the boarding house. There they found out that the boarding mistress was in a hospital and that a girl scarcely more than their own age was in charge.

"Yes, Mr. Greene left just a short while ago," said the girl. "He had gotten word that an aunt of his was sick and that he would have to go and see her immediately."

"Did he say where the aunt lived or what her name was?" asked Randy.

"Why, he said the aunt lived in Rochester and that her name was Sobber—Mrs. Arabella Sobber."

"Did he say when he would be back?"

"No. He said that would depend entirely on how he found his aunt. If she was very sick he might stay there quite a while." And this was about all the girl could tell them.

"Evidently Ken Greene doesn't hesitate to tell fairy tales when it suits his purpose," was Andy's comment when he and his twin were again on their way back to the offices in Wall Street. "Said he was going to Rochester and then takes a train for Galveston! Some little distance between those two places, if you ask me!"

"Did you catch that name—Sobber?" returned his brother. "That sounds familiar to me. I've heard my father mention that."

"Tad Sobber was one of the rascals who tried to do Aunt Dora and her mother out of the fortune that was left by Mr. Stanhope. Sobber and a fellow named Sid Merrick went down to Treasure Isle and did their best to get the treasure in their possession. But their ship, the *Josephine*, was caught in a hurricane and went down with everybody on board excepting four sailors who escaped in a rowboat and were picked up in a steamer bound for Havana. Since that time Tad Sobber and the other rascals have never been heard of."

"But if this Ken Greene is really related to the Sobbers, that would certainly make him no friend of our father, and especially no friend of Uncle Dick."

"Probably not. In that case, Greene would most likely be only too willing to do an injury to those who had kept his relative from getting a whack at that money."

The older Rovers listened with keen interest to what the twins had to relate and asked many questions concerning Greene. Then one of the detectives from the private agency was called in and he immediately took up the task of following this new lead.

In the meantime something else had happened at the homes on Riverside Drive which looked to Fred and Jack as if it might be of importance. Randy and the others had taken their undeveloped photographic films to a shop in the neighborhood, and now Mary and Martha, out for a walk, had brought the finished pictures back. In looking these over, Fred and Jack came upon the snapshot Randy had taken just before the touring car with the broken mudguard and broken headlight had bowled Andy over in the roadway and injured him.

It was a fairly good picture, only one corner of it being slightly light struck. It showed the groundhog passing under the back wheel of the touring car. The car itself seemed to have a big dent in the back. Two men were on the front seat and one fellow was in the rear. The latter had just turned around, evidently to gaze at the boy who was using the camera, so that his face was turned full toward the lens.

"It's Nelson Martell!" exclaimed Jack, in amazement. "Nappy's father! What do you know about that?"

"You're right!" said his cousin. "And that being so, more than likely one of the other men in the car was Slogwell Brown, for they always travel together, just like their sons."

"This picture was taken after the hold-up at the offices. I wonder if there can be any connection between these two happenings."

"I don't know. But I should say that it would be a good thing to have the Martells and the Browns watched."

When the others got home they examined the photographs with interest. Then the twins told the other boys of following Ken Greene and of how they had discovered he was a relative of their fathers' former enemy, Tad Sobber.

"It certainly begins to look as if some of our old enemies were mixed up in this affair," was Tom Rover's comment. "The question is, how are we going at it to prove it?"

"The only thing I can think of to do is to place the detectives and the police in possession of all the facts," said Dick Rover.

"All sorts of things are piling in just now," came from Fred's father, after a slight pause. "I got a telegram from Captain Oran Corning that he would be at the house to see me either this evening or the first thing in the morning."

"Oh, Dad, is he coming about that hunt for the *Margarita*?" cried Fred.

"Yes, but I'm afraid that I'll have to disappoint the old captain. I'll have to give my entire attention to this hold-up business now," said Sam Rover.

"I suppose that's right," came rather dolefully from his son. "Too bad! And just after I've been telling the other fellows all about it and we thought it would make a dandy outing for the crowd!"

"Anyway, it won't hurt to listen to the old captain's yarn, will it?" asked Randy, who was eager to know more concerning the lost steam yacht.

"No, it won't do any harm to listen to what Captain Corning has to say," was the reply. "Just the same, it will be a bitter disappointment to the captain if we let him tell his whole story and then tell him that we can't take part in the search he wants to make. He, of course, wants us to finance the hunt, or at least put up the larger part of the money that would be necessary. He has some funds, but not enough to see the affair through."

Dinner was over and the boys and the men had just gotten together again when a servant came in and Captain Corning was announced.

CHAPTER XIX
CAPTAIN CORNING'S STORY

CAPTAIN ORAN CORNING WAS a heavy-set man with a round and exceedingly pleasant face. He had a hearty voice, and the boys had listened to him less than ten minutes when all felt that he was very sincere and all liked him exceedingly.

"Yes, I heard about that hold-up in Wall Street," said the captain in reply to a question from Sam Rover. "I can't understand why the police can't get after those fellows and round them up. Why, those bandits are worse than the old-time pirates used to be!"

"Of course you understand, Captain, that this affair has upset us very much," went on Fred's father. "And it has completely changed many of my plans."

"Well, I thought that might be so. But then I got to thinking that maybe you'd be more eager to go on the hunt for the *Margarita* than ever. Since I was talking to you I've got some additional facts concerning that wreck and the value of the things on board of her, and I believe it would be a better speculation for you to help me find the wreck than some of these speculations you fellows go into in Wall Street."

"We're not speculators, Captain," put in Dick Rover. "That is, we do not take anything more than regular business risks, the same risks that all business men have to take. We do not deal in any securities of the wildcat order."

"Oh, yes, yes, I understand that! And you'll excuse me, Mr. Rover, if I was a little too blunt. But what I meant is that I'm pretty sure that we can locate that wreck, and, if we can, everybody who puts up his money in this expedition will get his share."

"How much do you think was on board the *Margarita* when she went down?" asked Fred.

"Well, of course, the exact amount is more or less problematic. I have found out that when Miguel Torra made his escape he had not less than fifty thousand dollars in gold with him and he had with him gold and silverware and jewelry and precious stones amounting to at least one hundred and fifty thousand dollars more."

"Gracious! Two hundred thousand dollars!" exclaimed Randy. "If we got hold of any such sum as that it would help out The Rover Company a whole lot!"

"Go slow, son! Go slow!" admonished Tom Rover. "Don't count your chickens before you've even got the eggs."

"Yes, but, Dad! if there is even a fair chance of locating this lost steam yacht, don't you think we ought to take it?" pleaded the youth.

"Certainly! But I would want to know a little more about what I was trying to do."

"I won't promise to go into this affair, Captain Corning. Not that I don't trust you, but because this affair in Wall Street needs my attention," remarked Sam Rover. "However, I'd like very much to hear what you have to say. And let me add that my son here and my three nephews are also greatly interested. These boys were once shipwrecked in the West Indies and fell in with an old sailor, and between them they managed to locate a pirates' treasure which, while it was not tremendously large, still gave each of them a snug little sum of money."

"Well, lads, if that's the case, you ought to be just the young fellows to help look for the *Margarita*," and Captain Corning smiled broadly.

"I wouldn't like any better fun," said Andy promptly. "An ocean trip always did suit me right down to the ground."

There followed a conversation lasting over an hour, during which time Captain Corning unfolded his plans while the boys listened eagerly and even the men were interested, though they could not get their minds altogether off of their financial troubles.

According to what the captain had to tell, Miguel Torra had set sail from a small port near Vera Cruz in Mexico at a time when a revolution was just coming to an end and he was very much in disfavor with those in authority. There had been a fight and it was not definitely known how many on shore and on the steam yacht had been killed or wounded. Then the yacht had sailed eastward with the evident intention of landing somewhere in the West Indies or on the upper coast of South America. But there had been mutiny and a great storm, and from what the captain had been able to learn from an old sailor who had since died in a seamen's home down East, the *Margarita* had been driven on either a sandbar or the rocks off the coast of Yucatan.

"As near as the old sailor could figure it, the spot was directly north of a place called Vera Sura."

"But isn't it very deep in the Gulf of Mexico?" asked Jack. "When we studied geography I remember there was one place there where the water was terribly deep."

"That's true, lad. But along the coast of Yucatan it's quite shallow and there are numerous sandbars and submerged rocks. So I have come to the conclusion that if the *Margarita* is really there, she may be in water from twenty to one hundred and fifty feet deep."

"How did this old sailor, Henry Swall, come to tell you all this?" asked Sam Rover.

"I helped the old fellow financially. I rather liked him, and I got him into the seamen's home. And not only that, I also helped his old mother who was blind. That made Swall very grateful and that is why he gave me all these particulars. He had hoped to go on a search for the *Margarita* himself. Before he died he signed a paper in which he left everything he had to me."

"Well, all this certainly sounds very interesting," mused Sam Rover. He turned to the boys. "It's just the kind of a hunt you'd like to go on, isn't it?" he added, with a little smile.

"You bet it is, Uncle Sam!" cried Andy.

"And just think of how much good that money would do us if we could get hold of it!" added his twin.

"Well, Dad, if you thought it was a good thing to go into, why don't you let us fellows go into it on our own account?" asked Fred. "That is, unless you think we ought to stay here and put in our time trying to solve this hold-up mystery."

So far Jack had not spoken and now his three cousins looked at him inquiringly.

"I hardly know what to say," said the oldest of the boys. "Of course, if we can be of any assistance around here we ought to stay. On the other hand, if there's a real chance of winning out in this hunt for the lost steam yacht, I'm in favor of going on the hunt."

"Would you be willing to put your own money in it, Jack?" asked Fred. "I'll put up every cent I've got."

"So will I!" came from the twins.

"Of course I'll put up my money! We certainly wouldn't expect our folks to do it. In fact, haven't we already offered our money to them?"

"Are you sure there is no one else who could claim a right in this *Margarita* if she was found?" asked Dick Rover.

"There isn't a soul who could make a claim so far as I've been able to learn," said Captain Corning. "This affair, you must remember, happened a good many years ago, when Henry Swall was only a young man. He was over seventy-five when he died last year. So it isn't likely that anybody would come forward and make a claim. You must remember too that the vessel was abandoned at sea, and that would make her the property of whoever found her."

"I believe you said you were willing to put up some money in this affair yourself," said Fred's father.

"I'm willing to put up every cent I can rake and scrape together," said the captain quickly. "That amounts to seven thousand dollars."

"How much money do you think you ought to have to see it through successfully?"

"Well, we've got to charter a vessel and take along a professional diver or two and perhaps take along a diving bell, too. We may have to do a lot of exploring before we hit the right spot and we may have to use dragnets and things like that. Also we'll have to have a competent crew and proper provisions, and all those things nowadays cost real money. I have figured out that we ought to have a backing of at least twenty-five thousand dollars."

"That means that you want eighteen thousand dollars in addition to what you can raise yourself?" asked Jack.

"Yes."

"Eighteen thousand dollars divided between the four of us fellows would be four thousand five hundred dollars apiece!" cried Randy. "I'd be willing to put up that much right now!"

"Ditto here!" said his brother.

"So would I be willing to put it up!" cried Fred. "But I'd want to go on the hunt too."

"Oh, of course, we'd want to go along!" came simultaneously from the twins.

"If you fellows put up your money, I'd do the same," said Jack. "But as things are now, I really think we ought to hold off for a few days before we decide on this." He turned to his father. "Don't you think so?"

"Perhaps it might be as well, Jack. You boys may be able to be of assistance here, although I can't just now see in what way you can help us. The police are doing everything they can and we now have three private detectives on the case. The detectives have a better chance of doing something than any of us have, if the criminals are our old enemies, for all our enemies know us and of course would get out of sight and become suspicious as soon as they saw us."

"And if the bandits were all outsiders, as they may be, then we wouldn't have much of a chance of tracing them," added Randy.

"But about our money?" went on Fred. "Are you quite sure, Dad, that you don't want it in your business?"

"Eighteen thousand dollars wouldn't help us very much, Fred," was Sam Rover's reply. "And if you boys really want to go on this hunt for the *Margarita*, as far as I'm concerned I'll say do it and use the money for that purpose." As he spoke he looked at his two brothers and Dick and Tom nodded in approval.

After this Captain Corning went into more particulars of what was in his mind to do, mentioning a vessel he could charter for the purpose, and telling of the professional diver and others he might engage for the trip.

"Gee, we ought to have old Ira Small along!" cried Andy.

"I don't think he'll go," said Fred. "I thought of him before. But he's now in an old sailor's home and not feeling extra well; so I think you'll have to count him out."

"I'll tell you what let's do," said Jack finally, after talking the matter over with his father. "We'll leave this whole matter rest for two or three days and then give Captain Corning a definite answer;" and so it was decided.

CHAPTER XX
THE DOTS IN A TRIANGLE

TWO DAYS WENT BY, and so far as the general public knew the affair of the hold-up had come to a standstill. The police authorities and one of the private detectives were working on such clues as they could pick up in and around Wall Street and among such professional hold-up men as could be rounded up, while two of the private detectives were following up all the clues vouchsafed by the Rovers concerning their various enemies.

"I've heard that you've had another enemy named Dan Baxter," said one of the detectives to Dick. "What about him?"

"Dan Baxter reformed years ago and he has now quite a reputation as a successful traveling salesman. He has a son, Walter, who was a chum of our boys when all of them went to Colby Hall. I don't think the Baxters had anything to do with this."

"Well, we want to get all the leads we can," was the detective's reply.

From one of the police detectives the Rovers gained quite some information concerning the two bandits known as Lefty Ditini and Black Ronombo. These fellows, who had lived both in Mexico and in Havana, Cuba, were very crafty criminals and were wanted for a long chain of crimes both in the West Indies and Mexico, as well as in some of our Southern states, notably Louisiana and Texas.

"It's only within the last year that these two rascals dared to come North and work in Philadelphia and New York," explained the detective. "They're both small and dark, and as hard boiled as bandits come."

"Well, our bookkeeper says two of the men were small and dark," said Dick Rover; "so it's just possible you are on the right track. If so, go to it, by all means, and round up these two rascals as quickly as you can."

"I only wish I could!" was the reply, and the detective heaved something of a sigh. "There are rewards aggregating forty thousand dollars for the capture of Ronombo and rewards aggregating half that amount for the capture of Ditini. I wouldn't like anything better than to capture that sixty thousand dollars!"

Mr. Stevenson had returned from his fishing trip and he appeared at the offices of The Rover Company that afternoon. Only Sam Rover and his brother Tom were present. Dick having gone to one of the banks to see what could be done in the matter of extending a loan which would come due in a few weeks.

"This is an outrageous state of affairs!" said Ruth's father, and his whole manner showed that he was in anything but an amiable frame of mind. He was having a great deal of trouble with the contractors who were laying out his estate at Dexter's Corners and, more than this, his fishing trip had been unproductive of results.

"It is certainly exceedingly unfortunate," said Sam, as he offered the newcomer a chair.

"Where is Richard Rover?"

"He's out on a little business. He'll be back in about an hour."

"I can't understand why these offices were left completely unprotected and why so many securities were left where the bandits could lay their hands on them," went on Mr. Stevenson, dropping into the chair and fanning himself with his straw hat. "I've read all the accounts in the newspapers. Somebody must have been grossly careless."

"Well, it's not the only hold-up that's happened in New York lately," said Tom, nettled by the visitor's manner. "Of course, if we had dreamed that we were going to have a visit from such bandits we would have been better prepared to meet them. It's too bad, and no one can be more sorry about it than we are."

"And then about that insurance! The idea of letting it lapse! Why, I never let an insurance policy lapse in my life!"

"That was the fault of one of our clerks. He did it either through carelessness or by design. Just now we're inclined to think that it was done deliberately, for the sole purpose of injuring us."

"Oh, say, Tom Rover, don't put it off on one of the clerks. Those things ought to be attended to by one of the officers!" Mr. Stevenson mopped his brow with his handkerchief. "How is this hold-up going to leave the Company?" he went on abruptly.

In as few words as possible, Tom and Sam explained the situation and told their new stockholder what they had done and of the loans and extensions they were trying to obtain. While this was going on, Jack's father came in and then the four men talked the matter over.

Presently Ruth's father calmed down a little and showed that he was a little ashamed of the irritability he had first showed. However, he still insisted that the lapsing of the insurance policy on the securities was due to sheer neglect on the part of the officers of the company and intimated that it was up to them individually to make good any loss that was sustained thereby.

"We're going to make the loss good if we possibly can, Mr. Stevenson," said Jack's father quietly. "It's a heavy blow to us, but we hope to be able to weather it. Many of our old friends have come to us and assured us of their assistance, and that means a great deal."

"Well, you can't look to me for anything more," returned Ruth's father. "With my investment of fifty thousand dollars in this company and a further investment of a like amount in that estate up at Dexter's Corners, I'm about as deep in financially as I want to go. Even as it is, if this loss down here isn't made good I don't know whether I'll be able to finish the house up there or not." And a little later Mr. Stevenson took his departure, declining Dick's offer to take him up to the house for dinner.

"He's sore—no two ways about that!" was Tom's comment after the visitor had gone. "He's as sore as a boil."

"Well, you can't altogether blame him, Tom," said Dick. "If we go to the wall he stands to lose fifty thousand dollars, one-half of which belongs to his wife. And, as he says, he may have to sacrifice some of the money he's already put into the estate in the country."

"Just the same, I thought he'd be a little better sport," was Sam's comment.

That evening Jack heard that Ruth's father was in New York and had called at the offices. When he heard from his father and his uncles of what Ruth's parent had said he was more disturbed than ever.

"If he doesn't get his money back he'll never forgive us," Jack told himself. He had not forgotten how Mr. Stevenson had acted towards his relative, Barnard Stevenson, on Snowshoe Island when the boys were there for a winter outing. Then he thought of how Ruth and her mother had acted and his heart grew heavier than ever.

That night one of the detectives called at Dick Rover's home with news that was decidedly interesting. He and one of his men had gotten on the trail of some men who had been found acting suspiciously on the Ten Brooks Road above the city on the evening of the day that the offices had been looted. From an old woman who lived on the road near a dense woods they learned that these men had been seen leaving one automobile and getting into another. The old woman had said that one of the men carried a square japanned box and that another had a similar box which was striped red.

"A box striped red!" exclaimed Dick Rover. "Did she say how large the box was?"

"Yes; it was about two feet long, four or five inches high, and four or five inches wide. The old woman thought it had a small brass lock at one end."

"Then this may be a real clue!" exclaimed Jack's father. "Because one of our new stockholders, Mr. Stevenson, brought his securities in a black box of that size which was striped red at either end. He left the box with us, and this was missing, along with one of our black boxes, after the hold-up."

"Then those rascals were undoubtedly either the bandits or in cahoots with them," said the detective.

"Did the old woman tell you anything else or did you find any other clues around the car?" asked Dick Rover.

"Nothing of any consequence. We had the car jacked up and mended sufficiently to run it to a garage a few miles away, and there it now stands."

When the boys heard of these new clues all were anxious to see the car that had been abandoned in the woods.

"I remember the old auto the Martells had when Nappy went to school, and I remember the car Slugger Brown's folks used," said Randy.

"And I remember those cars too," said Fred. "What do you say to going up and inspecting the old bus?"

Getting out one of their own automobiles, the next morning the four boys made the run to Ten Brooks Road and to the garage where the old car was stored. They found the place in charge of an old man who gazed at them curiously as they entered.

"We came in to look over that car that was brought in from the woods," explained Jack. "Mr. Lawson said we could inspect it."

"There she is," said the old man, and pointed to a car resting in an adjoining shed.

The automobile was a two-seated open affair and had evidently seen hard service. Both the mudguards and the sides, as well as the rear, were dented and the cushions were torn in several places.

"Looks as if it had about come from the ark," was Andy's remark.

"An old model, but one with a fine engine," returned Jack. "I'll bet this old bus could make forty or fifty miles an hour easily."

"Well, those hold-up men would probably want something that could make speed," said Fred.

The boys looked over the car with care, but for some time discovered nothing out of the ordinary about it. Then, however, Jack found in the pocket of one of the doors several sheets of paper, on one of which appeared a number of dots put down in the form of triangles.

"Hello! what do you know about this?" exclaimed the oldest Rover boy triumphantly.

"What is it, Jack?" came in a chorus from his cousins.

"I think I've got a clue!" was the reply. "See these dots placed in the form of triangles? Well, look around the car and see if you can find any more of them."

Feeling sure that their cousin had discovered something of importance, the other boys made a minute inspection of the car, aided by Jack. Presently Fred pointed out a series of dots on the dashboard, evidently made with the point of a knife blade. These dots also were in the form of a triangle.

"And here's another one on the top of the back door!" cried Randy. "Jack, what in the world does this mean?"

"Don't you remember who used to make these dotted triangles?" asked the oldest Rover boy. "Put on your thinking caps and go back to your school days at Colby Hall."

All of the lads stared at him in wonder and then dropped their eyes and began to think deeply. Then suddenly one after another they set up a shout:

"Slugger Brown!"

CHAPTER XXI
THE BOYS REACH A DECISION

IT WAS WITH GOOD reason that the Rover boys mentioned Slugger Brown's name in connection with the discovery they had made. All remembered clearly how the bully of Colby Hall had had the habit of placing dots in a triangle, not only while in the classroom but also when discussing affairs at the gymnasium meetings and while at the military school encampments.

"It's undoubtedly the work of Slugger," said Jack. "I've seen him put down those dots in triangles hundreds of times."

"It's more than likely this old auto belonged to Mr. Brown," came from Fred.

"Maybe he was with the men who had the security boxes," ventured Randy. "One thing I feel pretty sure of—this hold-up was engineered by our old enemies."

"It certainly begins to took that way to me," said Jack. "First we spot Slugger Brown and Nappy Martell watching us. Then we discover Mr. Martell in the automobile that knocked Andy down, and here we find this auto, that was used by the men who had the two security boxes, marked with what you might call Slugger's absent-minded hieroglyphics. I begin to think if we can lay our hands on that bunch we'll be pretty close to getting the stolen stuff back."

The other boys agreed in this, and it looked to them as if the whole affair solved itself into the single question of locating the rascals who formerly had made so much trouble for themselves and for their parents.

The lads lost no time in returning to New York. There they reported what they had learned and this revelation was listened to with much satisfaction by their fathers.

"These things are beginning to fit in," said Tom Rover. "I certainly hope those detectives are able to round up the Browns and the Martells."

But this was by no means easy. An investigation proved that both families had moved away from where they had formerly lived, and a thorough search by not only the Rovers but also half a dozen detectives failed to give a hint as to their whereabouts.

"It begins to look to me as if the bunch had left this country," said Tom Rover.

"Have the police heard any more regarding Ditini and Ronombo?" asked Randy.

"If they have, they haven't reported it. They still are of the opinion, however, that those two noted bandits had something to do with the crime."

"It might be so, Uncle Tom," came from Jack. "I don't believe the Browns or the Martells would have nerve enough to do the actual hold-up work themselves. They may have been in cahoots with these bandits."

"Perhaps." Tom Rover heaved a sigh. "I don't care so much who did the trick. What I'm interested in is in getting our securities back."

That day Jack received a short letter from Ruth. In it the girl stated that she was very sorry that the hold-up had occurred and that she sympathized deeply with the Rovers in their loss. She added that her mother was still sick from the shock and that her father was much depressed, not only on account of the hold-up but because he was having considerable trouble with the contractors who were building the new country home. She added that she made no plans for the rest of the summer and did not intend to make any.

It was a rather matter-of-fact letter, neither particularly cool nor particularly warm, and Jack hardly knew how to take it.

"I guess she thinks she has got to side with her mother and her father in this," he mused. "Well, I can't exactly blame her; it must have been a great blow to all of them."

In the meantime Captain Corning was growing impatient to start his hunt for the missing steam yacht. He said that some other people had gotten hold of the story of Miguel Torra and the sunken *Margarita*, and he was afraid that they would organize another expedition and get ahead of him.

"I've had two or three parties come to me and hint that they would help me out financially if I'd divide with them," said the captain to Sam Rover and the boys. "But I want to give you the first chance because you've been very nice about this and I sympathize with you in the trouble you've had."

This brought on another long talk in which Dick Rover and Tom also joined.

"I don't see but what you boys might go on this search for the *Margarita*," said Sam Rover. "I can't go because I must stay here in New York. Your Uncle Dick has got to go down to Texas and see about an oil deal we've been putting through, and your Uncle Tom has got to go out to the Rolling Thunder mine because he's received a hint that that Peter Garrish has been making trouble again."

"Well, if you're sure we can't do anything here—" began Jack.

"I don't see what you can do," put in Dick Rover. "The Browns and the Martells have completely disappeared and it isn't likely that you could find them any quicker than the detectives who are on their trail. The police authorities are hunting for Ditini and Ronombo, and what more can be done I don't know. You might as well go on this hunt for the steam yacht, and we can do our best to keep in communication with you, in case anything turns up and you're needed."

More talk followed, and before the meeting broke up it was agreed that the four boys should accompany Captain Corning on the hunt for the missing *Margarita* and that they were to furnish the additional eighteen thousand dollars which the captain needed to finance the expedition. In return for this, it was agreed that if anything of value was recovered, after all necessary expenses were paid the balance was to be divided into three parts, one part going to Captain Corning and two parts to the Rover boys; these to be divided equally between the youths.

Captain Corning was a first-class seaman, but frankly admitted that he did not like to keep any books or do any direct financing, so it was agreed that Fred should become the secretary for the expedition and Jack should act as treasurer.

"That leaves Randy and me free to become real sailors!" cried Andy gayly. "Captain Corning, we'll be at your service," and he touched his forehead in true salt-water fashion.

"All right, lads, I may take you up on that," said the captain, smiling. "I'll ship a full crew, but there's no telling what work there'll be to do when we locate the *Margarita* and try to get at it." He liked the boys as much as they liked him, and that was one reason why he had been so anxious to get them to go on the search for the sunken steam yacht.

"We'll draw our money from the bank to-morrow," said Jack after consulting his cousins. "Then we'll take that amount and what you're to pay in, Captain Corning, and place it in a special account to be drawn on whenever needed. I'll make out the checks and we can fix it so you can countersign them if you wish."

"I know an honest young man when I see him, Mr. Rover," said Captain Corning quickly. "I don't think the checks will need any countersigning."

The next week proved a busy one, not only for the captain but also for the boys. The captain had a list of vessels available for charter and allowed the boys to go with him to look over the various craft, which were located in New York Harbor and along the Long Island coast. They at last settled on an oil-burning yacht named the *Firefly*, the property of a rich cotton merchant who was now on a tour around the world.

"She's certainly a dandy looking craft," remarked Jack, as he and his brothers walked around the boat, a yacht nearly two hundred feet in length and rather broad of beam. "She looks as if she could stand real service, too."

"I'm glad she doesn't look too fancy," said Fred. "There may be a lot of rough work to do if we ever do locate the *Margarita*. This isn't just an outing for fun, you know."

There were several sailors already attached to the *Firefly*, and these men readily agreed to sign up with Captain Corning for the trip. Then the captain obtained several men who had sailed with him before, including a mate named Nat Brooks, a man well acquainted with the Atlantic seacoast and the West Indies. It was known that the expedition was on a treasure hunt, but no details were mentioned.

Some newspaper reporters heard of the affair and at once imagined that the Rovers were going after those who had held up the offices in Wall Street, and Jack and his cousins allowed them to think this and smiled to themselves when they read an account in the various journals that evening.

Captain Corning had thought to get two divers with whom he was acquainted to go with him on the hunt, but at the last minute found neither of these men available. This was a keen disappointment, and he did not know what to do next. Then his mate came to him and said that one of the sailors, a Norwegian who had sailed on the *Firefly* before and now signed up for the trip, knew of another Norwegian who was an expert deep-sea diver and who had just finished a contract with one of the lighthouse corporations.

"Peterson says this diver, whose name is Leif Olesen, is a very reliable man," said Brooks. "He's worked both for the Atlantic Lighthouse Corporation and for the Hazlett-Dockery Company, laying both lighthouse and bridge foundations. If he's done all that, perhaps he's just the fellow we want."

"I'll look him up and have a talk with him," said the captain.

As a result of this, Leif Olesen was engaged, along with his helper, another Norwegian named Nick Amend. Both were tall, fair-haired and blue-eyed, and both seemed to understand their business thoroughly. The captain told Olesen just what he had in mind to do, and the deep-sea diver gave him a list of what ought to be taken along and of what sort of equipment he himself would need.

After this began the task of provisioning the *Firefly* and having the tanks filled with oil, and while this was going on the boys spent part of their time at their homes getting ready for the trip.

"We won't want much heavy clothing, that's sure," said Randy. "I'll bet it's as hot as pepper down there this time of year. We ought to start this hunt during the winter months."

"Yes, and let somebody else get ahead of us, eh?" put in Fred quickly. "Nothing doing! The sooner we locate the *Margarita* the better I'll be pleased."

"I'll bet Fred has his profits counted up already," gibed Randy. "Remember, Fred, after all expenses are paid you're to have one-quarter of two thirds of three-thirds," and he grinned gayly.

"You don't have to poke fun at me, Randy Rover!" cried his cousin. "You're just as anxious as I am to find this treasure!"

"Sure he is—we all are!" put in Jack. "You don't suppose we put up eighteen thousand dollars just for the fun of it?"

"And if we don't locate the *Margarita*, then it's good-bye to the eighteen thousand," came from Fred.

"Don't mention that we may lose that eighteen thousand!" cried Andy. "Not on top of all our folks have lost! That would be too mean for anything!"

"Well, this treasure hunt is a gamble, Andy; you know that as well as I do. We may be successful and we may lose every dollar we put into it."

CHAPTER XXII
BOUND FOR THE GULF OF MEXICO

"OFF AT LAST!"

"Good-bye, everybody! Take good care of yourselves!"

"Good-bye, boys! I hope this quest proves successful."

The time for the departure of the *Firefly* had come at last. The oil-burning yacht was leaving from one of the docks in Brooklyn, and all of the other Rovers had come over to see them off.

"Be careful and don't let anything happen to you!" called Martha Rover.

"And be sure to send us letters whenever you get a chance," put in Mary.

"Don't lose any hairpins, Mary, while we're gone!" shouted back Andy, in an attempt at light-heartedness, for he could see that the girls, as well as the boys' mothers, were looking very sober. Of all things, Andy detested seeing a girl or a woman cry.

"Be careful and keep out of trouble," called Dick Rover. "And if you need any assistance don't hesitate to send a wireless or a telegram."

"We'll be all right, Dad!" shouted Jack. "Good-bye, Mother! Good-bye, everybody!" Then, while the boys and men waved their caps and hats and the girls and the ladies waved their handkerchiefs, the *Firefly* slid slowly out of her berth by the side of the dock and turned down the East River toward the Bay; and the expedition in search of the lost *Margarita* was begun.

Jack hated to leave his folks, but there was another pang in his heart which, however, he took good care to keep to himself. He had risked a telegram to Ruth, stating that he was going on the quest, and he had hoped for some sort of reply in return. But up to the hour of sailing no word had been received from the girl who was so dear to his heart.

And up to the hour of sailing no additional information had come in concerning those who were supposed to be responsible for the hold-up in Wall Street. Not a trace of the Browns or the Martells, nor of Ditini and Ronombo, had been received. So far as could be ascertained none of the securities stolen had been offered for sale. Evidently the bandits and all in league with them were keeping well under cover or else they had left for foreign parts.

All of their baggage had been sent to the *Firefly* the day before, and the boys had arranged with Captain Corning regarding the staterooms they were to use. These rooms were two double ones on one side of the cabin of the yacht. On the other side were staterooms used by the captain and his mate. There were other staterooms further back, and these were assigned to Leif Olesen and his assistant, Nick Amend.

The boys had met the head diver twice, and he appeared to be a man who understood his business, but also a fellow who was far from sociable. But as the diver had not been hired for his society, this lack of sociability counted for nothing with them.

"All we want of him is to locate the wreck and get up the treasure for us," was the way Fred had expressed himself. "If he'll do that, he can look as sour as he pleases."

It did not take the yacht long to run down into the Bay and past the Statue of Liberty, and that evening found them on the rolling waters of the Atlantic heading southward along the New Jersey coast.

"Hope we don't run into any more bootleggers," was Randy's comment. He had not forgotten the trouble occasioned by doing this at the time they had tried to make their way in a motor boat from Nantucket to Cape Cod, as related in "The Rover Boys Shipwrecked."

"Well, we'll have to take what comes," said Jack.

Only a few fishing vessels came anywhere near them. A coastwise steamer from the south was in the offing, but kept several miles away.

Not to be short-handed in case there was work to do in trying to raise the *Margarita* or to get what was aboard the sunken steam yacht, Captain Corning had shipped a crew of twelve men, so that there was little or nothing for the Rover boys to do while the vessel was plowing on her way southward. They visited the engineer and his assistant, and also looked in on the cook in the galley, and even took short turns at the wheel in company with the captain and the mate.

"Looks to me as if we were going to have the best kind of weather," remarked Fred to the mate, on the second day out.

"I hope so," said Nat Brooks. "But I'll tell you more about it later."

"Why? Do you think there is a storm approaching?" asked the youngest Rover boy quickly.

"I know we're getting into waters where you can't tell much about anything," was the reply. "You know the old saying, don't you, about the calm before the storm? Well, this may be such a calm. If you'll notice, there's scarcely a breath of air stirring. If it wasn't that we have our engines going, we wouldn't be making any sort of headway."

"Yes, I noticed there wasn't much wind. I hope it doesn't blow too hard. We were wrecked down here once, and I wouldn't like to be wrecked again."

"Oh, don't worry about that, lad. The *Firefly* is a staunch yacht, with first-class engines, and it would take nothing short of a hurricane to send her over or on to the rocks."

With so little to do, the boys spent quite some time looking over the charts and maps which Captain Corning and the old sailor, Henry Swall, had drawn up in trying to locate the sunken *Margarita*.

"Here is a chart of the northern coast of the state of Yucatan, Mexico," said Captain Corning. "As you can see, this state is really at the upper end of Central America and directly on the southern coast line of the Gulf of Mexico. In the center of the Gulf, the water is very deep—two or three miles, in fact. But along the coast of Yucatan it shallows rapidly, and there are many sandbars and rocky elevations where the water is less than a hundred feet in depth. Now, Henry Swall was pretty sure that the *Margarita* went down on a sandbar opposite the village of Vera Sura, a place which was afterwards burned and which has since been abandoned. According to this latest chart, which is a Mexican document, the water there is not over forty or fifty feet in depth. If that is so, we ought not to have any great difficulty in locating the wreck, providing, of course, the shifting sandbars haven't covered her."

"If this chart was made by the Mexicans within the last few years, wouldn't they be liable to find the wreck in making their soundings?" asked Jack quickly.

"They might, lad. But I've made careful inquiries concerning that, and I can find no government report of the *Margarita* having been located."

"But if the center of the Gulf is so very deep, wouldn't the wreck be apt to slide down from the shore line into the hole?" asked Andy.

"That could happen, my boy. And that, of course, is one of the risks we're running. My hope is that the *Margarita*, when she went down, either got caught in the sand close to shore or otherwise got caught on some rocks so she couldn't slip. Of course, if she slid out into the Gulf and down into deep water, why, our search for her will avail us nothing."

"But we've got a diving bell! We could use that!" cried Fred.

"Not if she went down a mile or two, Fred. Divers can go down to a certain depth, but as yet they've discovered no means of going down as far as that. The water pressure is too great."

It was at this point that Leif Olesen came in and joined in the conversation. The Norwegian spoke fairly good English, although with a strong accent.

"I've been on two other hunts for lost ships before this," said the deep-sea diver. "One off the coast of Norway and the other off the coast of Nova Scotia.

In Norway we found the ship and brought everything up that was of value. The job took four months, and for my work I received about two thousand dollars."

"Well, I've promised you more than that, if you're successful this time, Olesen," said the captain.

"What of the second ship you went after?" asked Jack.

"There we were very unfortunate. We located the ship and worked for ten days to turn her in the sand so that we could get at the things in her cabins. Then a fierce storm came up and we had to run for safety. When the storm was over we went back and hunted everywhere, but the wreck had disappeared, and although we sailed and searched around in that vicinity for a week we were unable to find the slightest trace of her."

"Gee, that was tough luck!" murmured Randy. "To have it snatched away just when you thought you had it."

"Well, that's the luck of the sea," said the diver. "You have to take things as they come," and he shrugged his shoulders and his face took on a sour look.

When the boys retired that night the yacht was pitching and tossing far more than at any time since they had left home. A breeze had sprung up, and this was increasing steadily.

"I shouldn't be surprised if we got a storm before long," remarked Jack, as he took a look at the sky. The stars had been out, but now the heavens were gradually becoming overcast. The wind commenced to whistle through the riggings and the boys could make out the dim outlines of whitecaps on the waves around them.

"Do you know, Jack," said Fred, when he and his cousin had retired to one stateroom and the twins had retired to another, "I can't say that I like that fellow Olesen at all! And I can't say that I like his assistant, Nick Amend, either!"

"He certainly doesn't strike me as being very pleasant, Fred," was the reply. "But just the same, from the way he talks, I guess he understands his business."

"Did you notice how eager he was to take in every word that Captain Corning has to say about the treasure? When the captain let slip as to its possible value I saw a light in Olesen's eyes that I didn't like. It was like a miser might have when he was gloating over his gold."

"Well, I suppose the fellow thought it was a shame that he couldn't pull up that treasure for himself. Nobody likes to dig up gold for the other fellow;" and there the talk came to an end.

The boys turned in, but as it was a hot night in spite of the ever increasing breeze none of them could sleep. Fred and Jack tumbled and tossed in their berths, and so did the twins.

"Gee, I can't stand this any more!" cried Andy at last. "I'm going to get up and go on deck. I'm sure it's cooler there."

"I'll go up with you," said his brother. "I'm fairly smothered down here."

Slipping on their sneakers and donning light coats over their pajamas, the two boys left their stateroom, walked through the cabin, and mounted the companionway.

"Some blow coming on now!" cried Andy, as they came out on deck to find the *Firefly* pitching and tossing in the fierce wind. "I guess we'll cool off all we want to and then some," he added grimly.

To get out of the worst of the wind, the boys made their way to the side of the upper cabin. Here there was a corner between the cabin and the yacht's funnel, and here were a couple of deck chairs where they proceeded to make themselves comfortable.

They were sleepy and had almost dozed off in spite of the wind and the pitching of the yacht when Andy, chancing to look up, saw three figures approaching. They were Leif Olesen and two of the sailors.

The three men were talking in Norwegian, but occasionally said a few words in English. Andy listened for several minutes and then caught his brother by the arm, at the same time placing his hand over Randy's mouth.

"Listen!" he whispered into his twin's ear. "See those fellows over there? They are Olesen, the head diver, and two of the sailors that were on this yacht when Captain Corning chartered her. They're talking about the treasure we are after, and I think they're up to some trick!"

CHAPTER XXIII
CAUGHT IN A STORM

AROUSED FROM HIS SLUMBER, Randy was inclined to cry out in alarm. But with his brother's hand over his mouth he made but little noise, and this was drowned out by the whistling of the wind which kept increasing steadily.

"Wa-what did you say?" stammered Randy.

His twin repeated his words and pointed out where Leif Olesen was in earnest conversation with two Norwegian sailors, one named Larsen and the other Smader.

"You think they're up to some trick?" whispered Randy.

"I certainly do! Let's catch as much of their talk as we can."

Such a suggestion was easily made but by no means easy to carry out, for the wind made much noise as it whistled through the rigging of the yacht and the rolling and pitching of the vessel made it necessary for the twins to hold fast to whatever was near them to keep from pitching headlong and taking the deck chairs with them.

Fortunately the backs of the three men were towards the lads, so they were not discovered. The men continued to talk earnestly, only raising their voices when the noises around them compelled them to do so.

As said before, most of the conversation was in Norwegian. Yet all of the men had been in the United States a number of years and they occasionally said a few words in English, and to these the youths listened with close attention.

"They're talking about the treasure, all right enough," whispered Randy. "But, for the matter of that, I suppose everybody on the yacht has mentioned that subject many times since we started on the expedition. I suppose they're all expecting extra wages if we find anything of real value."

"Just before I woke you, Randy, Olesen said something to the other men about 'We want our share, don't we?' That's why I woke you up. I tell you that man has got something up his sleeve."

Presently as the wind increased and it was evident that a storm was coming up, the three men moved away, and soon after that the boys saw Leif Olesen go down the companionway, evidently bent on retiring.

"Hello! what are you fellows doing on deck?"

The greeting came from Nat Brooks. The mate had been called up by the man in charge of the wheel, he having given orders to that effect should the blow increase.

"It was too hot below for us," said Randy. "We thought we'd come up and cool off a bit."

"Well, you be careful you don't blow overboard."

"Looks like a storm to me," put in Andy.

"Yes, I think we're going to be up against some dirty weather," said the mate. "However, I think the *Firefly* will pull through all right enough. She's one of the most substantial craft I ever sailed on."

The boys remained on deck a half hour longer and then, growing more sleepy than ever, went below and turned in. By this time the storm was on the yacht and from the southward came streaks of lightning followed by long rolls of thunder.

"Gee, how the thunder does roll on the ocean!" was Randy's remark, as his head hit the pillow.

"I don't care, let it thunder. I'm going to sleep," said his twin. "The air is changing and it's much cooler."

"It's only the wind. I don't believe the thermometer has dropped one point."

Fred and Jack had managed to go to sleep. But less than half an hour after the twins retired a second time all of the boys were wide awake, and with good reason.

The *Firefly* was pitching and tossing in the teeth of what seemed to be little short of a hurricane. Jack all but rolled to the floor and had all he could do to stand upright. Then came a crash on the partition separating the stateroom occupied by himself and Fred from that used by the twins, and this was followed immediately by a yell from Randy and a burst of laughter from Andy.

"Something went wrong in there, that's sure!" cried Fred. "Let's get a few clothes on and see how bad this storm is getting."

The boys donned their sneakers and also their trousers and coats, and then Jack and Fred went to join their cousins. They found Randy sitting on a stationary stool rubbing his elbow and Andy sitting on the lower berth laughing at him.

"Randy has been trying to do circus stunts," explained the twin's brother. "He got out of the top berth because he couldn't sleep any more, and then he crawled back to find his cap that I had thrown up when we went to bed. Just then the yacht gave an extra heavy lurch and he slid right off the top berth and went kerbang into the partition."

"Yes, and I almost went through the woodwork," came ruefully from Randy. "Hit right on my elbow, too! Gee, I'll bet it's black and blue!"

"Well, be glad it wasn't your head," said Fred, who could readily see that Randy was not much hurt. What really did hurt the twin was the fact that his brother was laughing at him, for an instant later he grabbed up a pillow and hurled this at Andy's head, following it an instant later with a shoe.

"Hi! Hi! Stop the bombardment!" cried Andy, in mock terror. "Don't you know the war is over and nothing is left of it but the debts? Stop, I say!" and he dodged behind Jack.

"Listen! We've got something to tell you," said Randy suddenly and thereupon he and his twin related what they had heard when they had gone on deck to get the air.

"Well, there may be something in that," said Jack slowly.

"And on the other hand we may be doing Olesen an injury," put in Fred. "I don't think I'd find fault with him until I had more evidence."

"Then you don't think you'd speak to Captain Corning about this?" asked Andy. "He's really the head of the expedition, you know."

"Oh, I think we'd better wait, Andy," said Jack. "We'll keep our eyes wide open and see what that head diver and his friends do."

Conversation now became more difficult for the boys had all they could do to keep on their feet as the *Firefly* pitched and tossed in the height of the storm. Everything that was loose in the staterooms was either flying around or otherwise already on the floor.

"I'm going up and take a look around," declared Jack.

When the boys went out into the cabin they encountered Captain Corning who was also going on deck. Ordinarily the captain would not have shown himself, having every confidence in his mate. But the yacht was new to the commander, just as it was also new to his first officer, and the captain thought it the better part of wisdom to inspect the *Firefly* and see how the craft was standing up to the storm.

"If you young men go on deck, let me warn you to be careful," said the commander of the yacht. "I don't want any of you to be blown overboard."

"We've been in storms before, Captain, and we'll take care of ourselves," said Jack.

When the boys got on deck they found it almost impossible to keep their feet. The wind was blowing wildly first in one direction and then in another. The waves seemed mountainous and occasionally one would break over the bow of the steam yacht, sending the spray flying in all directions.

"Free shower bath, and then some!" was the way Andy expressed himself. "We'll either have to go below again or put on oilskins."

The storm lasted until an hour after the time when the sun should have come up, and during that time sleep was out of the question. But around nine o'clock the clouds began to break and two hours later the wind died down and by noon the sun was shining as fiercely as ever on a sea that still showed many whitecaps.

"Well, we're out of that, and I'm glad of it," said Fred, as the lads went down to dinner. "Now we can eat in comfort and after that I'm going to have a good snooze."

The remainder of that day and also the next passed without special incident. The steam yacht was now getting well down the coast and it would not be long before they would be in the vicinity of the West Indies.

Among the sailors Jack had noticed a tall, lean individual, named Patnak. This fellow was of Norwegian birth, but told the oldest Rover boy that he had been in and around the United States since he was twelve years old. He was thoroughly Americanized, and although he could speak Norwegian he had little or nothing to do with the two sailors who had become friendly with Olesen and Amend.

Jack rather liked Jake Patnak and felt he could trust this Norwegian who, although he was all of thirty years old, acted very much like an overgrown boy. He told Patnak of some of the adventures he and his cousins had had, not only in the West Indies but also in the oil fields and on Sunset Trail, and thereupon Patnak became quite confidential.

"Every year I tell myself that I'm going to leave the sea and try to make my fortune on land," said the sailor, his blue eyes full of earnestness. "Once I started for those oil fields that you just mentioned, but after I was ashore for three months the itch for the ocean again got me, and inside of three days I had gone back to Baltimore and signed up for a cruise to Cape Town, Africa."

"Well, every one to his taste," said Jack. "You can't hire some men to go on the water."

"I know that. When I was on land I met two Norwegians who had come over to this country when I did. They were experts at laying parquet floors. Why, those fellows wouldn't even go down to Coney Island for a swim, they hated the water so," and Jake Patnak laughed.

"You seem to be more like an American than a Norwegian," remarked Jack.

"I'm a full-fledged citizen and I vote whenever I have the chance to do so," said the sailor, a bit proudly. "I have very little desire to visit the old country. I love the sea and love to take trips upon it, both short and long. But if I ever settle down on land it will surely be in the United States."

"Is Leif Olesen a citizen?" asked Jack, just for the purpose of bringing the conversation around to the deep-sea diver.

"No. He has never taken out papers, so he says; and he doesn't intend to. And his helper, Nick Amend, isn't a citizen either."

"What about these other Norwegians on the yacht? Do you know anything about them—I mean the fellows who were on the *Firefly* when Captain Corning chartered her?"

"I don't know much about those fellows. You see, I came aboard with the cap'n and Mr. Brooks. I sailed with them on two other trips, and I liked 'em so well that I told the cap'n and the mate both that I'd stick to 'em as long as they wanted me."

"Well, I'm glad to know that, Patnak," and Jack's face showed his satisfaction. "You know, on a trip like this we want all our friends to stand by us," and Jack looked at the sailor suggestively.

"Yes, Mr. Rover, I understand that." Thus speaking Patnak drew a step closer. "You and the cap'n can depend on me, no matter what happens."

Jack could readily see that the sailor had more in his mind than his words conveyed. He looked at Patnak sharply.

"Do you think anything is going to happen?" he asked. "I mean anything out of the ordinary?"

"Who can tell?" Jake Patnak shrugged his lean shoulders. "If we're not successful, then, of course, everything will go along all right."

"But if we are successful—"

Jake Patnak stretched himself, filled his lungs with air, and blew his breath out vociferously.

"If we were successful that would be another story, Mr. Rover, especially if the treasure found was a large one. Gold and silver and jewelry and precious gems are a great temptation to some people, you know."

Here the conversation was interrupted by the approach of two other sailors, one of whom told Patnak that he was wanted by the mate. Then all of the sailors went off, leaving Jack in a thoughtful mood.

CHAPTER XXIV
A MESSAGE OF IMPORTANCE

Jack lost no time in communicating with his cousins, and the four boys talked the matter over again and then decided to speak to Captain Corning about it.

"You know the old saying, 'Forewarned is forearmed,'" declared Jack. "We'd be in a fine pickle if we allowed that diver and his cronies to do us out of the treasure if we found it!"

Fred took the message to the captain, telling him they wished to see him in private and on important business. All repaired to the rear deck where they might be free from interruption.

Captain Corning's face was a study when the lads told of what they had heard and Jack had related Patnak's views on the subject.

"There may be nothing in this, and on the other hand it may mean a great deal," said Captain Corning. "Personally, I must confess that I don't like Olesen nor do I like Amend, and yet they came very highly recommended, and that ought to count for something. I'm glad that you spoke to Patnak and I'm sure that he'll stick to us, no matter what happens. I never met a sailor I liked better, and Mr. Brooks likes him too."

"What do you think of those other Norwegians—the fellows who were aboard the *Firefly* when you chartered her?" asked Randy.

"They seem to be good enough sort of sailors. If they hadn't been I wouldn't have let them sign up with me. But, of course, that class of fellows is often easily influenced by others. In fact, you can easily influence lots of sailors. When a proposition is put up to them they reason that they have very little to lose and everything to gain. Most of them don't own a thing outside of what is in their chests and their ditty bags. If Olesen was really contemplating getting his hands on that treasure for himself, it might be an easy matter for him to start a mutiny on board and get some of the men to stand in with him simply by promising them a nice share of the loot."

"My gracious, what a pack of rascals there must be in this world!" sighed Fred. "If the head diver and his bunch did that, they wouldn't be any better than those bandits who held up the offices in Wall Street."

"Well, you know what some men say of life," returned Captain Corning, smiling grimly. "They say it's a fight to get something and after that it's a fight to keep it."

"Well, what do you think we ought to do, Captain?" asked Jack.

"We can't do anything yet outside of keeping our eyes and ears open. If we discover any real plot on Olesen's part to start a mutiny, I'll have the *Firefly* taken to the nearest port and we'll hand him and his followers over to the authorities. But we can't do anything like that until we've got sufficient evidence."

"Would it be a good plan to ask Patnak to keep his eyes and ears open and report to you?"

"It might be, Jack, because I think he's perfectly honest. On the other hand, if he should take it into his head to play in with those other Norwegians, then it would be the worst possible thing for me to do, because then he could double-cross me, as they call it. I'll think it over. And, in the meantime, I'll speak to Mr. Brooks and I'll ask you to keep your eyes and ears wide open, but don't let Olesen and the others notice that you're watching them. If they find that is being done, they'll become more secretive than ever."

Before leaving on the trip it had been decided that the *Firefly* should stop at Key West for a day or two to get into communication with those left behind. Accordingly, the course of the steam yacht was set in that direction. After the storm the weather became somewhat cooler, for which all aboard the *Firefly* were thankful.

"Now we can sleep nights," was the way Randy expressed himself. "And believe me, I'm going to do it!"

During the remainder of the run to Key West all of the boys kept their eyes on Leif Olesen and Nick Amend. But this produced no results.

"We either misjudged them or else they're playing foxy," declared Jack. "Olesen has talked to those two Norwegian sailors only twice, so far as I've been able to learn, and then the conversation didn't seem to have anything to do with the treasure. They were talking about the birds that are flying around the ship and about wanting to get something to drink when we arrive at Key West."

On signing up for the trip there had been one bit of friction between the two divers and Captain Corning. This had been on the subject of liquor which the captain would not allow on board.

"I've always had a sober crew and I always intend to have," was the way the captain expressed himself. "I can't stop you when you're ashore, but I don't intend to have any drunkenness on my ship!" and this rule he carried out with everybody who sailed under him.

The run down the coast of Florida interested all the boys, for at some spots they drew quite close to the shore. Here they were once stopped by a government vessel looking for rum runners, but were soon let go with an apology from the officer in charge of the small boat which boarded them.

"Too bad we didn't have a little rum on board," said Nick Amend, making a wry face. "A drink just now wouldn't go bad."

"Well, we'll get something good when we go ashore at Key West," said Leif Olesen.

"You'd better go slow on bootleg liquor," was Captain Corning's advice. "Remember a deep-sea diver needs to keep his eyesight."

"Oh, I know good liquor when I see it," grumbled Amend.

Just before they landed at Key West, which, as my readers must know, is located on the extreme southern point of Florida, Fred, walking forward on the deck, caught sight of Olesen behind the foremast in earnest conversation with Larsen and Smader. The three were talking in Norwegian, and, as before, only an occasional word was spoken in English. But these words interested Fred deeply, and he listened attentively until the sailors had to go off to attend to their duties and the diver walked to the stern. Then the youngest of the Rover boys rushed off to join his cousins.

"Here's a new one!" he exclaimed excitedly. "I just caught Olesen talking to those two sailors, Larsen and Smader. He mentioned pistols and ammunition several times, and so did one of the other men!"

"Pistols and ammunition!" exclaimed Jack and the twins simultaneously.

"That's what!"

"Sounds bad to me," went on the oldest of the Rover boys. "Looks as if they were surely getting ready for a mutiny."

"Don't you think we had better tell Captain Corning?" came from Randy.

"I certainly do," said Jack. "What do you think, Fred? You heard them talking."

"I think Captain Corning ought to know all about it, and at once."

After this the lads lost no time in hunting up the commander of the *Firefly*, who was talking to one of the dock officials.

"Humph!" mused the captain, after Fred had told his story. "That certainly does look bad! I think I had better have Olesen and Amend watched while they're ashore and find out just what they do."

"We'll keep our eyes on them if you say so, Captain," said Jack promptly.

"I'm afraid that wouldn't go, Jack. Those fellows know you and your cousins too well. I'll fix it up—never fear. I know the officials down here and know a number of other men too. I'll have some strangers keep tab on them."

It had been arranged that the boys should stop at a local brokerage house known to the elder Rovers and there receive any mail or messages that might have come in. So, telling the captain that they were bound for that place, they leaped into a taxicab and were soon on their way.

"Gee, I wish we could have followed up Olesen and Amend and caught them in the act of supplying themselves and those other Norwegians with firearms!" was Randy's comment as they rode along. "If those fellows are up to some underhand work I'd like to catch 'em right in the midst of it."

"And that's just what I'd like to do!" put in his twin.

"Well, we can't be in two places at once," came from Fred. "I'd like to watch them too, but I'm also anxious to get some letters and messages from home. If they have managed to round up those hold-up men I want to know it."

"Oh, well, I want to know that too!" came promptly from Andy.

"Now that we've warned Captain Corning I guess we can trust him to have those fellows watched," said Jack. "He's as suspicious of them as we are and just as anxious to save that treasure, provided it's located."

It did not take the taxicab long to reach the offices of Ditson and Roebuck, the brokers known to the Rovers. When they entered the place a round-faced, good-natured clerk came up and shook hands cordially with them.

"I remembered you the minute I saw you, Mr. Rover," he said to Jack. "Don't you remember I was in your office in New York one day—the same day you had had trouble with the son of another broker named Martell?"

"Oh, yes! I remember you now, Mr. Ditson!" cried Jack. He knew that the young man was the son of the head of the firm.

"We're after letters and messages," put in Fred, a bit impatiently. "We trust you've got good news for us."

"I don't know how good it is," was the reply, as Harry Ditson walked back of one of the counters and brought forth a number of letters and several telegrams. "I certainly hope they've been able to get track of the stuff that was stolen from your firm. My! that was rather a serious affair, wasn't it?"

"We'll tell the world it was!" responded Randy, as he took a letter addressed to himself and tore it open eagerly.

Jack had two telegrams, as well as a letter. One telegram was from Ruth in which the girl stated briefly that she was very sorry she had not received his communication in time to answer it before the *Firefly* sailed and that she hoped the treasure quest would be successful. Jack read this telegram twice, and it is perhaps needless to say he was much gratified.

The other telegram was one from his father, evidently sent two days after the steam yacht had sailed. Dick Rover merely stated that all were well and that there was no news of importance and that he was making a hasty run to the oil fields while Tom Rover was going out West to the Rolling Thunder mine.

"Too bad that there is no good news from Wall Street," said Jack, after all had read the telegrams. Then the boys turned to the letters which had been written by Mary and Martha and the mother of the twins.

Mrs. Tom Rover and the girls had little of importance to tell except that all of the men were greatly worried because the banks were not inclined to renew some of the loans made to the Company. Dick Rover had said something about sacrificing some of his interests in the oil fields, and both Tom and Sam had mentioned that they might sell their interest in one of the gold mines.

"Looks to me as if matters were blacker than we thought," mused Randy. "It's too bad, isn't it?"

"If only we could locate that treasure and help them out!" murmured his brother.

After reading their letters carefully the boys had a little further conversation with Harry Ditson and were then on the point of leaving when a telegraph messenger came in.

"Hello! here's another telegram for you," exclaimed Harry Ditson, and turned it over to Jack.

The telegram was from Sam Rover and ran as follows:

Have located Josiah Crabtree and made him confess. Look for important developments in the near future.

CHAPTER XXV
SAM MAKES A DISCOVERY

WITH DICK ROVER GONE to Oklahoma and Texas and his brother Tom having taken his departure for the Far West, Sam Rover found himself in sole charge of the offices in Wall Street and consequently the only one to battle with a situation that was becoming worse every day.

Not to worry their wives and the young folks too much, the older Rovers had not told everything concerning the peculiar financial straits in which they were beginning to find themselves. These straits resolved not alone into difficulties brought about in the brokerage business because of the stolen securities but embraced also a deal made in the oil fields and two other deals in the mining districts of the Far West. Because of this peculiar situation, The Rover Company had to obtain at least four hundred thousand dollars inside of the next six weeks. Of this amount the banks and the firm's friends could be relied upon to furnish two hundred and fifty thousand dollars. But where the other one hundred and fifty thousand dollars was to come from, neither Dick, Tom nor Sam knew.

Up to within twenty-four hours of the time that the younger Rovers arrived at Key West nothing more had been heard concerning the bandits who had held up the offices. Both the authorities and the private detectives seemed to be doing their best on the case, but without material results. They had traced Ken Greene to Galveston and there lost track of the clerk. They had also traced the Browns and the Martells from the middle of New York State to Buffalo, only to learn that these individuals had without warning left that city for parts unknown.

"It's more than likely they escaped into Canada," said Sam Rover to himself when he received this news. "And if that's so, it will become more difficult than ever to trace them."

And then, while the youngest of The Rover Company officials was in the depth of despair, something happened which gave him information of the greatest importance. A retired broker whom the Rovers knew fairly well was stopping in town at a hotel near the Grand Central Terminal and Sam resolved to call on this man, thinking that possibly he might obtain an additional loan to carry on the business. Sam had come over from his home on Riverside Drive in the family automobile. On Forty-second Street near Fifth Avenue the car was halted by the police because of a fire in that vicinity.

"I'll get out and walk the rest of the distance," said Sam to the chauffeur. "You can remain here or otherwise turn back and park somewhere near Sixth Avenue."

There was great excitement in the street, and people were hurrying in several directions to clear the way for the fire engines. Sam found himself caught in the crowd which suddenly broke, and then a long hook and ladder truck came speeding toward him, the powerful motor making a fearful din as it advanced.

Close to Sam was an elderly man who limped slightly. He carried a cane and when the crowd broke this clattered to the roadway and the man seemed suddenly terror-stricken.

"Get out of the way there! You'll be killed!" yelled some one in the crowd.

Sam had leaped to safety, but now turned and saw the peril of the older person. He leaped forward once more, caught this individual by the arm, and dragged him backward just as the massive hook and ladder truck dashed madly by, the wheels just grazing the feet of the rescued one.

"Close shave for you," remarked Sam, as he stood the elderly man on his feet and picked up his cane.

"So it was!" panted the other. "I didn't think it was so close. I was—" Then, as the rescued one looked more closely at Sam, he stopped short, his mouth open in wonder.

"Josiah Crabtree!" ejaculated Sam, and again caught the man by the arm. "What are you doing here? You are just the man I want to see!"

"Don't touch me, Rover! Don't touch me!" pleaded the former instructor of Putnam Hall. "Don't touch me! I haven't done anything!"

It was plainly to be seen that Josiah Crabtree was just over one fear to have another come upon him. As his shifty eyes looked at Sam, his face became blanched and he trembled.

"You come with me," went on Sam somewhat sternly. "No nonsense now, or I'll call a policeman."

"No, no! Don't do that! Don't do that!" pleaded Crabtree, and he looked more frightened than ever. Evidently he had not forgotten his former terms in prison and he had no desire to give up his liberty again.

"Then come with me."

"All right, Rover, I will," was the ready reply. Then, with Josiah Crabtree's arm safely within his grasp, Sam led the way out of the crowd and to where his chauffeur still remained with the automobile.

"Now, Crabtree, I'll give you your choice," went on Sam, doing some rapid thinking. "You can either go home with me and talk things over or I'll call an officer and have you placed under arrest. Which shall it be?"

"You don't have to call an officer. I'll go with you. I'll tell you everything! Only, please leave me alone, Rover! I'm getting to be an old man now! I don't want to go to prison again! I was dragged into this thing! Otherwise, I wouldn't have had anything to do with it!"

"Then you're willing to admit that you had your share in the hold-up in Wall Street, eh?" went on Sam, anxious to follow up the advantage he saw he was gaining.

"I wasn't near Wall Street! I'm not that kind of a man—you know that," whined the former teacher. Evidently what little courage he had possessed was fast deserting him.

"But you had something to do with the affair."

"Well, it wasn't much. I was on the outside. I was hard-up and they promised me a thousand dollars if I'd help them. But I haven't had a dollar—not a cent!" groaned Josiah Crabtree.

"Well, come along," and without further ado Sam bundled the old man into the car and gave directions to the chauffeur to drive home as fast as he could.

It may be taken for granted that Grace Rover, as well as her sister Nellie, and Dora, were astonished when they discovered who the visitor was. None of them had forgotten how Josiah Crabtree had tried to harm them in the past nor the fact that the old man had spent two terms in prison.

"Just wait outside the door, Johnson," said Sam to the chauffeur. "And tell Rankin to go to the rear of the house. This man must not be allowed to escape under any circumstances. He's one of the rascals wanted for that hold-up."

Having given these orders, Sam went to the telephone and called up the private detective agency working on the case and asked that one or two of the detectives be sent up immediately.

"Now then, I want your story, Crabtree, and I want it straight," said Sam, after these details had been taken care of. "No phony work, now!"

"Will you promise not to prosecute me if I tell you all I know?" pleaded Josiah Crabtree, as he sank into a chair, his hands shaking violently on the top of his cane as he did so. "I'm an old man, now, Rover, and I haven't many more years to live, and I don't want to go to prison again. Spare me and I'll tell you everything."

"Then you're willing to turn state's evidence?"

"I am. I didn't want to go into this in the first place, but, as I said before, they promised me a thousand dollars and that was a terrible temptation because I had less than a dollar in my pocket at that time. But they didn't give me a cent!

This morning I was turned out of the rooming house where I was stopping, and all I've had to eat was one small ham sandwich washed down with a drink of water," and now the tears stood in Josiah Crabtree's watery and shifty eyes.

Had Sam not known this man as well as he did, he might have been sorry for the former teacher. But he knew how crafty and cruel Crabtree had been for many years, and so he did not allow the man's pleadings to soften him.

"If you get out of this with a whole skin it will simply be because you help us to round up those bandits and get back our securities," he said. "Otherwise you'll take your medicine."

"I'll do all I can!" cried Josiah Crabtree in the tone of a drowning man clutching at a straw. And thereupon he made a revelation which was so astonishing that Sam could hardly believe it at first. This revelation was repeated to the two detectives who arrived a little later, and then Josiah Crabtree was closely asked until nothing more could be extracted from the old man.

Crabtree revealed that the hold-up had been planned by Slogwell Brown, Nelson Martell and Ken Greene, the latter a nephew of their old enemy, Tad Sobber. Mr. Brown and Mr. Martell had had, of course, to take in their sons; and then Slugger Brown had met Crabtree when the latter arrived in New York and through the former teacher had been enabled to call in several other fellows, including Jerry Koswell, who had been the Rovers' enemy at Brill College, and Pelter and Japson, who had tried to ruin the Rovers when they had first established themselves in business in New York City.

Crabtree was not certain how Mr. Brown and Mr. Martell had become acquainted with the notorious hold-up men, Lefty Ditini and Black Ronombo. But these men had been called into the game and they in turn had had the assistance of several of their pals.

The hold-up had been planned a number of weeks before it occurred, and many of the details were carefully worked out. Slugger Brown and Nappy Martell were to see to it that none of the Rover boys came back to New York from Valley Brook Farm, and Josiah Crabtree had been utilized in sending the fake messages to Dick Rover and to Dora after the telegrams had been sent which had taken Tom and Sam out of the city.

"I know the hold-up came off successfully," said Josiah Crabtree. "And I know that Ken Greene got away from the offices without being exposed. I also know that Slugger Brown and his father met some of the bandits at the time one of their autos broke down and they had to transfer to another. But when I went after Mr. Brown and Mr. Martell to get what was coming to me, they declared that they had been double-crossed by Ditini and Ronombo and some of the others and that they hadn't got a cent of the loot and consequently couldn't give me what I had been promised. I thought they were fooling at first, but they insisted upon it that every cent of what had been stolen had vanished and they said they were going to skip out themselves before the officers of the law pinched them. I tried to get ten or twenty dollars from them just to tide me over, but they wouldn't give me a penny."

"Where did the Browns and the Martells go?" asked Sam.

"I believe they went to Buffalo. But they said something about Galveston Texas, and I shouldn't be surprised but what they went there. You see, these fellows, Ditini and Ronombo, were Mexicans, and I think they had an idea that the rascals would go to Galveston to a place where they used to visit and that they might have a chance of locating them."

This was as much as Josiah Crabtree could tell, and after he had been asked for several hours Sam and the detectives came to the conclusion that the former teacher was telling the truth so far as he knew it. He did not know what had become of Ken Greene and they did not enlighten him.

That evening the wires to Galveston were kept hot by the detectives who notified other detectives in the Texan city to be on the lookout for all those connected with the hold-up. But day after day went by, and no news of importance was received. Josiah Crabtree was given twenty dollars by Sam with which to tide himself over, but soon after he left the residence on Riverside Drive he was arrested on a technical charge of vagrancy and held by the police, thus making sure that he would be on hand when wanted.

CHAPTER XXVI
HIDDEN EVIDENCE

THE BOYS WERE GREATLY interested in the brief telegram received from Fred's father and they were sorry that they were not in New York City to learn the particulars of what was taking place.

"Gee, I hope they do clear up that affair in Wall Street!" sighed Randy.

"Yes, and I hope Uncle Sam gets all the securities back," added Jack.

The boys sent a telegram home stating that they were well and that they were going to continue the trip the following morning.

When they returned to the *Firefly* they found that Captain Corning, as well as the head diver and his assistant, had gone ashore. The mate was in charge and said that two of the sailors had had a brief leave of absence. It was not until late that Captain Corning returned, coming in shortly after the arrival of Olesen and Amend. The sailors did not come in until later.

"I had Olesen and his assistant followed," said the commander of the *Firefly* in response to questions from the boys. "They visited several questionable resorts where I suppose they got some bootleg liquor. They did not go near any hardware stores or other places where they might have purchased firearms. Just the same, they may have gotten some pistols on the sly."

"Olesen came aboard with a package," said Jack; "but of course I don't know what was in it."

The *Firefly* sailed early the following morning, the course being now southwest to the coast of Yucatan. The sun was exceedingly hot, but the heat was tempered by a fair breeze, for which all on board were thankful. Now that they were getting closer to the spot where the *Margarita* was supposed to be resting, the boys became more interested than ever in the drawing and charts which Captain Corning possessed, and pored over the papers by the hour, trying to figure out just where the ill-fated steam yacht had gone down. The captain and his mate, as well as Leif Olesen, likewise studied the papers and also studied several books which the captain had brought along, books that gave much information concerning the coast line of Yucatan and a study of the shifting sandbars and of such storms as occurred along this coast from time to time.

"We've got a pretty good idea of where the *Margarita* was abandoned," explained Captain Corning. "So the only question is: In what direction did the derelict blow after the craft was left to herself? Did she go up the coast or down, was she blown ashore or on a sandbar or the rocks, or did she slide down into the depth of the center of the Gulf?"

"Let's hope she went on a sandbar or on the rocks," said Fred.

"Yes, and that she is still there," added Andy.

"Well, boys, you mustn't be too much disappointed if we fail to find the *Margarita*," warned the captain. "I'll hate to lose my money, just the same as you'll hate to lose yours. But we've got to be prepared for a failure just as much as for a success."

Sunday passed quietly and two days later found the *Firefly* steaming slowly along the coast of Yucatan. The yacht had several drags out, drags which had been constructed by the head diver, and his assistant after consultation with the captain and the mate.

"After all it's a good deal like looking for a needle in a haystack," sighed Fred, as hour after hour went by without results.

"It won't do to get discouraged so early in the game, Fred," said the captain, with a grim smile. "If we go over a few miles of the bottom around here every day, we'll be doing very well."

From a section of the regular chart the captain had constructed a much larger affair, and this he had divided into numerous squares.

"We'll go at this thing systematically," he said. "We'll try to take one square at a time, and thus sooner or later we'll have a pretty good idea of what is on the whole bottom around here."

Once or twice other vessels came close, wondering what they were doing. But generally speaking, they were unmolested, several Mexican fisherman, however, gibing at them when they guessed they were looking for a treasure.

"Ha-ha! That's an old story," said one of them. "If you're lucky you may bring up some old anchors or sea boots, and that will be all," and, lighting a cigarette, he waved his panama hat and sailed away.

"Evidently those fellows don't believe much in a treasure," was Jack's comment.

Day after day went by and the search continued, but without results. Then the boys grew a bit depressed and so did the captain and his mate.

"Looks a bit like a wild-goose chase," was the way Nat Brooks expressed himself. "It seems to me we've been raking over miles and miles of Gulf bottom and got absolutely nothing for our pains."

"Well, we've covered twenty-two of those squares on the captain's chart," said Randy. "That's something."

"Yes, and there are only about seventy squares left," came from Andy. "We've got to hit something sooner or later," he added hopefully.

"If we strike something before the whole checkerboard is crossed off!" sighed Fred. He showed plainly that failure would mean a great disappointment to him.

And for the matter of that, failure would mean bitter disappointment to all. Even the captain was beginning to look worried and spoke rather sharply when he addressed the men. The seven thousand dollars he had invested in the quest was practically all the money he possessed.

Another day passed, and this was unusually warm, for the breeze had died away. The boys sat under an awning trying to keep cool and trying to amuse themselves by reading and talking.

Presently Jack grew restless and began to pace the deck. He went well forward and then, turning, found that Jake Patnak had followed him.

"Well, Jake, this is getting to be a long-winded affair," he remarked pleasantly to the tall sailor.

"Mr. Rover, I want to speak to you, but I don't want Leif Olesen or Nick Amend to see me," returned the tall sailor in a low tone of voice. "Come here, please," and he pointed to the side of the forecastle.

"What is it? Have you discovered something?" asked Jack, as he stepped to the place indicated.

"If I were you and the captain, I'd watch Olesen and Amend very closely," said the sailor, and his face showed his earnestness. "I think they've discovered something and they're not going to let you know what it is."

"You mean something about the treasure?" asked the oldest Rover boy quickly.

The sailor nodded.

"What was it?"

"That I can't tell you, because I wasn't close enough at the time to see. It was a couple of hours ago, when Captain Corning was below and Mr. Brooks was busy on the forward deck. Those two sailors, Larsen and Smader, were hauling up one of the drags and Olesen and Amend were with them. There was something on the end of the drag, a curious shaped thing over a foot long and maybe six or eight inches around and covered with seaweed. As soon as it came up the two divers looked at it carefully and then Olesen put it inside his jacket and went below with it. Maybe you had better ask Captain Corning or Mr. Brooks if they know anything about it. But if they say anything to Olesen or Amend, please don't mention me, because I don't want to have any trouble with them if I can help it."

"All right, Jake, I'll try to keep you out of it if I can," said Jack. "And I'm sure Captain Corning will do what he can for you, too. He told me he liked you very much."

"That so? Very good!" and Jake Patnak's round face beamed with delight. He was one of the kind of men who would never be anything but an overgrown boy.

It did not take Jack long to find the captain and tell the master of the *Firefly* of this new development. The captain said he would look into the matter without delay.

"If Olesen is hiding anything from me, he may have done that trick before," said the captain.

"But what good would it do him? He can't take the treasure away from us until it is brought up," replied Jack.

"He may be trying to play an old trick on us," was the captain's answer. "That trick is to locate the treasure, but not let us know anything about it. Then, after we've sailed away and given the quest up, he could come back with his own crowd and bring it to the surface."

"Do you think he's up to something like that now?"

"I don't know what to think. But I know he has no right to hide anything from me on board this vessel."

"Don't you think it would be more advisable not to say anything just yet? If you anger him he may throw up his job and go ashore and take what information he's now got with him. That would leave us in the lurch. Why not let him and his assistant go ahead and watch every move they make? Then, if he's doing any crooked work, we'll catch him red-handed sooner or later."

Captain Corning was a straight-forward man, and this "beating around the bush," as he expressed it, did not suit him at all. However, he took Jack's advice and talked it over with his mate, and Mr. Brooks agreed with the oldest Rover boy that they had better not say anything to the divers until more evidence against them was forthcoming.

"But I'll tell you what we can do," went on the mate. "When Olesen and Amend are on deck, we'll make sure that they stay there and then some of us can search their staterooms and see if they have anything hidden there that was brought up from the Gulf bottom."

"That's an idea," returned the captain. "We'll do it."

Jack told the other boys of what had taken place, and Fred and Andy were delegated to go on deck with Mr. Brooks and give warning if the two divers attempted to come below. Then Captain Corning and the other two boys went into Olesen's stateroom and began a hasty examination of its contents.

"I suppose he'd raise a terrible rumpus if he found us going through his things," said Randy.

"He can't raise any rumpus with me," declared the captain. "I am in absolute command on this ship, and I have a right to search every nook and corner if I want to."

"I know you have," said Jack. "But that wouldn't prevent Olesen from feeling sore."

The majority of things in the stateroom were of the ordinary kind, and in those the searchers took little interest. Then they opened Olesen's trunk, which was unlocked.

"Nothing here that looks as if it was taken out of the water," said the captain after a hurried glance through the contents.

"Wait a minute before you shove that trunk back," said Jack, getting down flat on the stateroom floor. "There may be something in the space behind it."

He felt in under the bunk as far as he could and presently discovered something wrapped up in an old newspaper. Both the paper and the object wrapped in it were wet.

"That shows that whatever the thing is, it came out of the water!" cried Randy triumphantly.

With eager hands the captain and Jack took the paper from the object, which proved to be a round wicker holder woven over an empty demijohn, the cork of which was missing.

"Well, why would he want to hide this?" asked Randy. "Why, it's only an empty liquor jug!"

"Here is why he hid it!" exclaimed Captain Corning, turning up the bottom of the wicker holder of the demijohn. "Do you see how this is stamped?" and he held the object closer to the light in the stateroom.

The boys looked, and then both of them gave a cry of astonishment. The wickerwork was plainly stamped with the name *Margarita*!

CHAPTER XXVII
THE MAN ON HORSEBACK

"This may mean a great deal and then again it may mean next to nothing," remarked Captain Corning, as all carefully examined the demijohn marked *Margarita*. "If it was found where the abandoned steam yacht rests, all right. But this demijohn may have floated for miles before it lost its cork and sank."

"Let's hope the spot where it was discovered marks the resting place of the *Margarita*," returned Jack. "Do you know where we were two hours ago? Jake Patnak said that was when it was hauled up."

"Yes, we can easily calculate the locality, or pretty close to it," was the reply. "I think I'll turn the *Firefly* back and see how Olesen and his assistant take it. I'll not say anything to the rascal until later."

The demijohn was hidden away once more and the stateroom put in order, and then all went on deck again. The necessary orders were given by the captain, and soon the yacht was headed in the direction from whence she had come.

"I thought we were going to keep on going eastward," said Olesen a few minutes later to Mr. Brooks.

"Captain's orders," was the brief reply.

If the head diver was suspicious, he gave no sign. However, a little later he went below and locked himself in his stateroom.

"He's going to take another look at the demijohn to see if it's still safe," remarked Jack.

Evidently Leif Olesen did more than look at the demijohn. When he came on deck again his face was red and he showed unmistakable signs of having been drinking.

"Looks to me as if this treasure hunt would amount to nothing," he grumbled. "I'm sorry I came on this trip. It's terribly hot down here."

"Well, any time you wish to quit, say so and I'll put you on shore," said Captain Corning sharply.

He apparently paid no more attention to the head diver, and the boys saw Olesen and Amend consult together. Then, when the ship sailed close to the spot where they imagined the empty demijohn had been hauled up, Fred and

Andy caught sight of Amend as he dropped something overboard. A little later they saw Olesen throw something into the waters of the Gulf.

"I wonder what that was!" exclaimed Andy. "Here, give me those glasses, quick!"

The boys had a pair of marine glasses handy, and as quickly as it could be done Andy adjusted these and gazed earnestly at the waters behind the yacht.

"I see something sticking up in the water. It's bobbing around like a little yellow flag."

"And that's just what it is!" cried Fred.

All of the boys looked at the object in the water and then hurried off to tell Captain Corning.

They found the captain in an exceedingly angry mood. The two Norwegian sailors, Larsen and Smader, were partly under the influence of drink and had admitted that they had received the liquor from Olesen.

"They're not going to play any more tricks on me," roared the master of the *Firefly*. "I'm going to run for the nearest town on the coast and put them ashore—I mean Olesen and Amend. The men can remain if they'll promise to keep sober and behave themselves."

"What do you suppose the yellow flag means?" asked Randy.

"I suppose it's some kind of a buoy. The water around here isn't over eighty feet deep, and he could easily attach a small flag to a large cork and then let down a line with a small weight attached. With a good pair of glasses the flag could be seen from quite a distance. Evidently those rascals intended to mark that spot. Probably they found something else besides the demijohn and feel pretty certain the wreck is somewhere in this vicinity."

The captain lost no time in carrying out what he had decided to do. He went below and armed himself and also armed his mate. Then he called Olesen and Amend to him.

There was almost an explosion when the head diver realized that his tricks had been discovered. He had just enough liquor in him to be ugly, and he was on the point of attacking the captain when the latter ordered him back, producing his pistol as he spoke.

"We're going to land at the nearest town, and both of you are going ashore," said the master of the *Firefly*. "I'll pay you off, and give you your passage money back to New York, and we'll let that end it."

Olesen wanted to argue the matter, and when not allowed to do this tried to become abusive. Then the captain told him to be quiet or he would be put in irons. Amend was scared and lost no time in going below to get his effects into shape to take away, and presently Olesen staggered down to his own stateroom.

Another storm was coming up, following the extra hot spell, and before they could make a landing it was blowing furiously. However, they got into a small bay in safety, and then Olesen and Amend were put off in a small boat for town, their effects going with them.

"You haven't heard the end of this!" roared the head diver, as he shook his fist when taking his departure. "Just wait and see what I'll do!"

"Hot air! Hot air!" shouted Nat Brooks after him. "You keep a civil tongue in your head or you'll never do any diver's work around New York again."

As soon as the divers were gone Captain Corning set sail once more, this time for a place further up the coast, called Progreso.

"I'm going to look for another diver," said he. "I understand that some of these Mexicans are very good at the game. This time I'll hire a fellow who'll do exactly what I order—no more and no less."

On going ashore at Progreso, from which a number of Gulf ships run to various points in the United States and the West Indies, the boys were delighted to learn that they could get into communication by telegraph and cable with the folks at home. And so, while the captain was busy trying to find another diver, they sent a message to New York.

It was not until three hours later that a reply came in. This was in code and had to be deciphered with care.

"Here is certainly news!" cried Jack. "Hurrah! They're getting on the track of those rascals at last!"

In the message Sam Rover told of Josiah Crabtree's revelations and of how the Browns and Martells and the others were being followed. Then came an announcement that was even more interesting to the lads.

> Antonio Ditini lived originally at Mendelopaz on the outskirts of Merida in Yucatan. Possibly he went home. Can you investigate?

"This is certainly remarkable!" cried Jack. "Merida is not many miles from here, and for all we know this Lefty Ditini may be there right now!"

"And don't forget that there is a big reward for his capture!" burst out Randy. "Gosh, I wish we could get hold of him!"

"If Ditini is in Yucatan we'll have to get some official to place him under arrest for us," said Fred.

"Yes, and we'll have to use some native for an interpreter," declared Jack. "I can't speak a dozen words of their language." All of the boys had seen pictures of Ditini and Ronombo in the Rogues' Gallery at New York City.

As Captain Corning was still away trying to hunt up another deep-sea diver, the boys consulted Mr. Brooks, who fortunately had been in Yucatan before and who could speak a little Mexican. As a result of this, they were introduced a little later to a Yucatan official who could speak fairly good English and who immediately became interested in the story they had to tell.

"I have an automobile handy," said the official, "and we can ride over in that. I think I'll have no trouble in locating the place where Antonio Ditini lives. Many folks must know this man who has become such a notorious bandit."

A little later the four boys and Captain Astora were on the way. The ride was anything but a comfortable one, but to this none of the lads paid any attention.

Arriving at Merida, the official made a number of inquiries and then learned that the wife of Ditini was living, as had been said in the cablegram, on the outskirts of Merida with her eight children. It was said that Ditini had deserted her, leaving her practically penniless.

"If Ditini is anywhere around I think I can make sure of it by letting his wife think that I must collect an old debt or throw her out of her home," said the Yucatan official. "Then, if he has brought money, or if he is expected to come with money, she will probably promise to pay."

It did not take the crowd long to reach the place where Señora Ditini lived with her many children, and while the boys kept out of sight in a grove of bushes the Yucatan official proceeded to put his trick into execution. He was gone the best part of half an hour, and when he came back his face showed his satisfaction.

"I tricked her very nicely," he declared. "I made her believe that she must pay me an old debt of four years' standing. She said she knew nothing of it, but would find out about it to-night. And she said further that she would surely have the money with which to pay by to-morrow morning. That proves to me that Antonio Ditini is either here or will arrive some time to-night."

The place was rather an isolated one, and, not to be discovered by any children or servants, the crowd drove away. Then the automobile was secreted in a nearby woods, and all went back to remain on guard.

Slowly the hours went by until night came on. They saw no one except two old Mexican servants and three or four children of various ages. Then, however, as it grew darker, they saw a man come up a side trail on horseback. He was a small, dark-skinned fellow dressed in Mexican costume.

"I'll wager that's Ditini," said the Yucatan official. "I'll go to the house and make sure. If I want your assistance I'll call you."

He walked rapidly toward the building and soon disappeared within. Ten minutes followed, the waiting boys growing more anxious every second. Suddenly angry words arose and they heard a woman cry out in dismay. Then followed two pistol shots. A moment later they saw a side door of the house burst open and the Mexican who had gone in but a short while before came rushing out, running towards where he had left his horse tied to a post.

"It's Ditini!" gasped Fred.

"He must have shot Captain Astora!" came from Andy.

"Come on—let's go after him!" shouted Jack. "We mustn't let him get away!"

CHAPTER XXVIII
THE MAN IN THE HAMMOCK

THE MEXICAN BANDIT HAD thought that the only person after him was Captain Astora, and he was taken completely by surprise when the four boys rushed up to him just after he had liberated his steed and was in the act of leaping into the saddle.

"Stop!" cried Jack, as he caught the horse by the bridle.

"Ha! Who are you?" demanded Ditini in his native tongue, and then, remembering that Jack had spoken in English, he repeated: "Who are you?"

"Never mind, Ditini! You get off that horse!" said Randy.

"American boys, eh?" sneered the bandit. "Get out of my way!" and he tried to urge his steed forward.

As he did this Fred and Andy rushed closer, one on either side of the horse. Each grabbed Ditini by a foot, and as a consequence as the steed made a plunge, in spite of Jack's effort to hold him, the bandit slid backwards and then came down to the ground with a thump.

"Let go of me, you little pigs!" roared the Mexican, as he lay on the ground. Then, as he scrambled to his feet, he tried to draw his pistol.

But the four Rovers knew that they had a desperate character with whom to deal, and they took no chances. Fred pounced on the rascal from behind, grabbing him by the throat, while Randy caught hold of the pistol before the man could get it from its holster. Andy threw himself on the bandit's legs, and Jack, letting the horse go, came forward and caught Ditini by the left hand.

"You might as well give in, Ditini," said the oldest of the Rover boys. "If you don't we'll knock you senseless."

For several seconds the bandit continued to struggle. But then, as Fred continued to choke him and Randy took away his pistol, he suddenly subsided.

"It's all a mistake. I don't know why you've attacked me," said he.

He had scarcely spoken when out of the house limped the Yucatan official who had received a slight flesh wound in his left thigh. He had his pistol in his hand and after him came Señora Ditini, begging loudly for mercy for her husband. The official had handcuffs with him, and soon Ditini was made a close prisoner.

The fellow was astonished when he learned who the Rover boys were and how it had been discovered that he and Ronombo had been the principal actors in the hold-up in New York City.

"But Ronombo is the man who got most of the securities," declared Ditini. "He did not divide with me as he promised. I was to have half, but he gave me less than ten thousand dollars!"

"Where is Ronombo now?" asked Jack.

"He went to his home in Nogistalia a few miles from here," said Ditini. "I hope you catch him! It will serve him right for the way he has treated me!" The rascal did not for a moment give consideration to the way he and Ronombo had treated the Americans who had been in the plot against the Rovers.

Captain Astora was in no condition to go after Ronombo, but managed to accompany the boys back to town, where Ditini was placed in custody. Then the four boys hired another auto and set out for Nogistalia.

"If only we can locate this Ronombo!" said Jack. He was trying his best to remember how the bandit looked.

"If he's so close, I don't see why Ditini didn't go after him for his share of the loot," said Randy.

"Well, perhaps we won't get to the bottom of this until everybody in the plot is rounded up," came from Fred.

They had received word concerning where Ronombo's people lived and arrived at the place some time after nightfall. They were directed to the proper house by a native, and then told the driver of the auto to wait for them and moved forward alone.

"We want to have our pistols ready," said Jack. "We'll take no chances on this fellow. They said in New York he was the more desperate character of the two."

They approached the house and heard the faint tinkle of a guitar and some singing by two girls. Then they moved around to where they saw a light and found an elderly man reading.

"Ronombo doesn't seem to be around," whispered Fred. "What shall we do—wait?"

"I don't think so," said Jack. "The news of Ditini's capture may travel fast, and if Ronombo hears of it, he'll lose no time in getting away. I think I'll try a ruse, just as Captain Astora did."

He walked up to the door of the place and knocked gently.

At first the old man who was reading paid no attention. But then he started and confronted his visitor.

"Hush! Make no noise," whispered Jack in a low voice. "Do you understand English?"

"A leetle," said the old man, his eyes staring in wonder.

"I have news! I must see Ronombo at once! Ditini is in the hands of the police!"

"Ditini captured? Who are you?"

"Ronombo knows me. I was mixed up in that affair in New York. I must see Ronombo at once. I guess you're his father, aren't you?"

"I am his grandfather. You say you took part in that affair in New York and that Ditini is under arrest? Ha, I told Gozo to be careful!"

"But where is he? I must see him at once! I can take him to a ship on the seacoast. We can go to Havana to-night."

"Ah, that is fine!" The old man's eyes showed his pleasure. "Come with me."

He led the way to the rear of the house and Jack followed. They went outside and as they advanced along a path, Jack motioned for his cousins to follow but to keep out of sight. They walked to a small house built at the end of a long garden. The place was of stone, cool and inviting. Here there was a hammock, and in this rested a small, dark-skinned man, his hat thrown on the floor.

The others had drawn closer, afraid that Jack might be walking into danger, and before the old man could say a word the oldest of the Rover boys clapped his hand over the old fellow's mouth.

"Grab him and don't let him make any noise," whispered Jack, and Andy and Fred understood and pushed the old man away from the summer house.

Ronombo was evidently exhausted and sleeping heavily. This being so, it was an easy matter for Jack and Randy to disarm him. From Captain Astora they had procured a pair of handcuffs, and these they slipped on the bandit just as he was awakening.

Black Ronombo's rage when he found himself a prisoner was indescribable. He almost foamed at the mouth and threw himself at the boys in a wild endeavor to annihilate them. He was not subdued until he had received several blows on the body and on the head and found himself menaced by the boys' pistols.

In the meantime, the old grandfather set up shriek after shriek which soon brought the two girls who had been singing to the spot, and likewise the driver of the automobile and some of the neighbors.

There followed a wordy war and for a few minutes it looked as if the Rover boys would be unable to take their prisoner away. The old man, as well as the girls, tried to fight them and had to be restrained by the neighbors and had it not been for the exhibition of firearms on the part of the Rovers there is no telling what would have happened next. But at last they got Ronombo into the automobile and then the prisoner was whisked away to town as speedily as possible.

"We've got to get a search warrant at once!" exclaimed Jack. "Not only for Ronombo's home but also for Ditini's."

This move did not come a minute too soon, for while it availed little at the Ditini place, it came just in the nick of time at the place where Ronombo resided. The authorities found the old grandfather hard at work in a cellar under the house and there was uncovered a fair-sized iron chest which, when opened, was found to contain about one quarter of the securities taken from The Rover Company's offices.

"Well, anyway, we've got that much," declared Jack. "Now the question is—what did these rascals do with the rest?"

Ditini and Ronombo refused to talk, but Captain Astora said he would make them speak later, indicating that he would have the bandits put through what is popularly called by the police "the third degree."

As speedily as it could be done word was sent to New York of what had been accomplished at Mendelopaz, Nogistalia and in Merida, and how the securities so far obtained were safe in a bank in the city. Then the folks at home were assured that the authorities would do all in their power to get from Ditini and Ronombo whatever was left of the rest of the loot.

"Well, we've got those two rascals and we've got between forty and fifty thousand dollars' worth of the securities they took," said Jack, when the excitement had somewhat subsided. "I call that a pretty good night's work!"

"It certainly is a good piece of work!" declared Fred. "Especially as there is such a good reward offered for the capture of those two bandits. Just the same, I hope we can get on the track of the rest of those securities. If not, it's going to be a terrible blow to The Rover Company."

The boys had communicated with Captain Corning and he at once came up from Progreso to Merida to see if he could be of any assistance.

"Of course if you boys want to stay here and see what the authorities can get out of these two bandits, you can do so," said the master of the *Firefly*. "But now that I have let Olesen and Amend go, I feel that I ought to continue the hunt for the *Margarita* without delay. If I don't, those fellows may organize a hunt of their own and get ahead of me."

"Well, I don't see what more we can do here," replied Fred, who, now that the excitement over the capture of the bandits had come to an end, was as eager as ever to look for the lost yacht. "I move we start on the hunt again and then come back here in a few days or a week and see what is doing."

"Did you manage to find another diver?" asked Jack.

"Yes. I ran into a fellow who came from New Orleans," said the captain. "A very fine chap named Barker. He says he'll be glad to go with me and do what he can, and at a reasonable price. He looks like a square man."

"Then let's continue the hunt!" came from Andy and Randy. And so it was decided.

CHAPTER XXIX
THE EXPLOSION

TWENTY-FOUR HOURS LATER FOUND the Rover boys once more on board the *Firefly*. Extra water and provisions had been procured and Captain Corning was accompanied by Fred Barker, the new diver, a middle-aged and rather silent man but one who was said to understand his business thoroughly.

Before leaving Progreso the boys had received another message from home congratulating them on what had been accomplished by them. Sam Rover sent word that he would at once communicate with the Mexican authorities and send two first-class men down to Yucatan to see what could be done toward locating such of the securities as were still missing.

"They'll probably get Ditini and Ronombo to talk when they put the screws on those rascals," said Jack, after this message came in. "Maybe the bandits placed the other stuff in hiding, thinking to let it remain there until this whole affair blew over."

So far the boys had talked of little else but the capture of the bandits and what this might lead to. But now, when they once more trod the deck of the *Firefly*, their thoughts again reverted to the hunt for the lost *Margarita*.

"We'll steam at once for the spot where that demijohn was found and where Olesen and Amend threw overboard the floating yellow flags," said Captain Corning.

It took the best part of the day to reach the vicinity the master of the *Firefly* had in mind. Then over an hour was lost before one of the tiny flags was located. It was pulled on board with care and they found the flag set in a piece of flat cork under which was a long fishline, at the end of which a small weight was attached, this intended to anchor it at the bottom of the Gulf.

Several drags were put overboard and they worked until nightfall in that vicinity trying to bring up something else of value.

But their efforts proved useless. Nothing was brought up but some seaweed and other marine plants, which the diver stated were quite numerous in that vicinity.

"Didn't even find another demijohn!" exclaimed Andy ruefully. "Tough luck!"

"What did you expect, Andy?" demanded Fred. "Did you think we were going to hit the *Margarita* first clap?"

The next day the search was renewed with vigor, and Barker made two trips under the waters of the Gulf. He took with him the most powerful searchlight of which the *Firefly* boasted.

"Nothing doing here," he announced. "There isn't a bit of wreckage in sight."

It must be confessed that the boys, as well as the captain, were rather disheartened by the diver's announcement and it was with heavy hearts that the search was continued the next day and the morning following. Then the mate announced that another storm was coming.

The blow reached them less than an hour later and the Rover boys noticed that Captain Corning was more than ordinarily interested as the storm increased in violence.

"It's just the kind of a storm that Henry Swall told me they had when the *Margarita* was wrecked and abandoned," said the master of the *Firefly* to the others. "I'm going to let the boat drift for a while and see where the storm takes us. That may give us some idea of what actually did happen to the *Margarita*."

A little while later the blow was on them in earnest, and with engines stopped the steam yacht drifted rapidly southeastward, heading for a part of the coast containing many indentations where there were rocks and sandbars, all backed up by a heavy tropical growth of trees, bushes and vines.

"We're getting toward shallow water now," announced Mr. Brooks a little later. "We'll have to be careful that we don't get on a sandbar or on the rocks."

The bottom at this point shelved gradually and now they were in water not over ten or twelve feet deep. The spot was noted with care by the captain, and then the *Firefly's* engines were started once more and they headed out into the Gulf in the teeth of the storm.

"Do you think that was the spot to which the *Margarita* drifted after she was abandoned?" asked Jack eagerly.

"Well, doesn't it look plausible?" was the captain's counter question.

"I'll say so—that is, if the wind was blowing then as it's blowing now."

The storm lasted until after midnight, but when day broke the sun came out as clear as ever and the Gulf was once more, comparatively calm.

They ran southward with care, taking many soundings so that they might not hit the rocks or run up on a sandbar. Thus they managed to reach a point not over a hundred yards from the shore and here anchored.

"We'll have to take to the gasoline launch," announced the captain, and this was done. Mr. Brooks was left in charge of the *Firefly*, much to his disgust, and the captain and the four boys, along with the diver and Jake Patnak, set off.

The remainder of the day was spent in moving in and out of innumerable coves. As they did this, all of the party kept their eyes open for some sign of the abandoned vessel. Once or twice they sighted some old wreckage, but this stuff proved of no value.

"Looks as if there was nothing to it, after all," sighed Fred, as they went back to the *Firefly* to spend the night. "Gee, I sure will be disappointed if we don't find something!"

The next morning they went out again, taking their lunch with them. The tank was filled with gasoline, and they told Mr. Brooks they would probably not be back before night.

The whole morning was spent in a search as useless as that of the day before. Then, tired out and more than warm, they sat down in the shade of some trees on the shore and there ate their midday meal, washing it down with the water they had brought along.

The land formation at this point was exceedingly irregular, and, having eaten and rested, Jack and Randy strolled off around the shore of a cove which, they presently discovered, opened into another cove.

The boys had moved along the shore of the second cove for a short distance when both of them set up a shout.

"There is something!"

"It's the wreck of a vessel!"

The shouts attracted the attention of the others and all came hurrying forward to learn what the cries meant. For answer, Jack and Randy pointed across the cove. Here there was a small sandbar and numerous trees and bushes, and half hidden by the latter rested a dismantled yacht almost ready to fall to pieces.

"It must be the *Margarita*!" exclaimed Fred joyfully.

"Come on, let's get over there as fast as we can!" came from Andy.

On account of the rocks and the thick jungle it would have been almost impossible to walk around the shore of the inner cove; so all rushed back to where the launch had been left and in a minute more they were on their way to the abandoned vessel.

"It's the *Margarita*, all right enough!" shouted Fred, as they approached. "There's the name as plain as can be!"

"Yes, it's the *Margarita*," said Captain Corning, and the tone of his voice was full of hope, yet his face showed keen anxiety.

"Looks as if somebody had been here ahead of us," was Jack's comment. "She looks as if she'd been stripped of everything of value."

"Oh, Jack, don't say that!" cried Fred, in dismay.

"Well, look for yourself. There isn't a bit of brasswork or an anchor or a chain left anywhere."

Telling the diver and Jake Patnak to remain on board the launch, Captain Corning led the way on board the abandoned yacht followed by the four Rovers. The yacht lay partly on her side so that walking on the deck was difficult.

"Be careful or you may break a leg or your neck," cautioned the captain. "There's a lot of rotten wood here, and you don't want to fall through into the hold."

As the boys advanced they grew more and more heavy hearted. They could easily see that the wreck of the *Margarita* had been visited many times and that almost everything of value had been carried off. The deck was practically bare and so were the cabin and the forecastle. Here and there lay bits of broken glasses and dishes, as well as water-soaked and moldy pieces of clothing and sailcloth. Down in the engine room the lighter parts of the machinery had been carted away.

"Well, I guess this is the end of the treasure hunt," remarked Captain Corning in a hopeless tone of voice.

"It certainly looks like it," returned Randy dolefully.

"You don't suppose Olesen was here?" asked Andy.

"Oh, no," said the captain. "Whatever has been taken away was taken long ago. I don't believe anybody has been around here for months."

"Let's take another look around," said Jack.

This was done, the new search lasting the best part of two hours. In the dirt they found a few small trinkets, the value of which would probably amount to several dollars.

"I've been thinking," said Jack, as they stood on the deck of the wreck, not knowing what to do next. "Wouldn't it be just like that fellow, Miguel Torra, to secrete the treasure so that the others on board couldn't get at it?"

"Well, we've looked into every place where the treasure might be put," said Captain Corning. "I even smashed in a part of that bulkhead in the bow and smashed down that pantry in the back of the cabin."

"I'm not in favor of leaving this wreck until we've made positive that there's nothing on board of value," declared Jack. "You told me you had a box of dynamite aboard the *Firefly*, didn't you?"

"Yes, lad, I did. I brought it along thinking we might have to blow the wreck up if the divers had trouble in getting into it."

"Well, why not blow this wreck up? Then we'll be sure that we haven't missed anything," went on the oldest Rover boy.

All agreed to this, and lost no time in getting back to the *Firefly*. Then the dynamite was transferred to the launch, along with the batteries and wires necessary for exploding the same.

Running with care, they presently returned to the *Margarita* and then, with the aid of the diver, who had handled dynamite charges before, the sticks of explosive were placed in various parts of the wreck and the batteries and wires were placed in position.

"Now then, we'll get behind the largest of these trees," cautioned the captain, "for there's no telling what that dynamite will do."

The launch was run to a safe spot and all took positions where they thought they would be well protected from the blast. A minute later Captain Corning pressed the button to set off the explosion.

There was a rumble and a roar and for the next fifteen seconds the air was filled with sticks of wood flying in all directions. and even the rocks and trees in that immediate vicinity were split and crushed.

"Gee, talk about the Fourth of July!" cried Andy. "That was the biggest noise I ever heard!"

"If there are any folks living around here they'll think it's an earthquake or something like that," added his twin.

Waiting to make certain that there would not be a second explosion, they moved forward with caution and soon stood close to the spot where the *Margarita* had lain. Split timbers and bits of woodwork lay in all directions and many of the pieces floated on the surface of the cove.

But neither the boys nor the captain were interested in these pieces of woodwork. With eager eyes they scanned one section of wreckage after another. Then Randy set up a shout.

"Look here! What's this?"

"An iron box!" came simultaneously from the others, and they rushed toward the object as speedily as their uncertain footing permitted.

"And here's another box!" came from Jack.

"Look yonder!" yelled Captain Corning, in intense excitement. "Gold and silver dishes, as sure as you're born!"

The master of the *Firefly* was right. There, amid the shattered wreckage, lay fully a score of elaborately engraved dishes and vases, a few of them silver and the others gold.

"That shows Torra hid his loot when he was aboard the yacht!" cried Jack. "And he hid it so well that up to the present time no one who has visited the wreck was able to locate it!"

They looked around further and in the end brought to light six iron boxes, as well as several other articles of gold and silver.

"Now to see what the boxes contain!" cried Jack.

The iron receptacles were much rusted. Each had two heavy padlocks, both of them locked.

"We'll have to take them aboard the *Firefly* before we can open them," said Captain Corning. Then without delay the transfer of the boxes and the silver- and goldware was begun.

CHAPTER XXX
HOME AGAIN—CONCLUSION

"GEE, SUPPOSE THE BOXES are empty!" murmured Andy while on the way to the yacht.

"If they were they wouldn't be so heavy," said Jack.

"And it isn't likely they'd be locked," added Fred.

They were soon aboard the *Firefly* and then Captain Corning had one of the men bring a cold chisel and a hammer, and with these implements the rusty and worn padlocks on the six chests were knocked off without great trouble.

A cry of amazement and delight burst from the boys when the covers of the various boxes were pried open and thrown back. There before their gaze was revealed a confused mass of gold and silver coins, jewelry, and many golden medals, and also eighteen small cases which when opened in their turn revealed articles set with diamonds and other precious stones. One case contained two strings of beautiful pearls and another a cross set in the finest kind of diamonds.

"This sure is a treasure, and no mistake!" was Captain Corning's remark as he gazed from one precious object to another.

"Worth real money, I'll say!" cried Fred, his eyes glistening.

"Worth thousands of dollars!" murmured Randy.

"I suppose those jewels and pearls are worth a small fortune in themselves," was Jack's comment. He picked up one of the strings only to have it fall apart, the pearls bouncing in all directions. And then all four of the lads lost no time in getting on their hands and knees to gather the precious objects together again.

It was a happy time and it was shared in by every man on board, even including the two Norwegian sailors who had been friendly with Olesen and Amend, for all of the men had been promised double wages and more by the captain should the quest for the treasure prove successful.

"Do you think we ought to land in Yucatan and telegraph to the folks about this?" asked Fred.

"I don't think I'd do that," returned Jack promptly. "If we went ashore, the Mexican authorities might put in some claim for this treasure, and we might have all sorts of difficulties in proving our rights to it."

"That's just the way I look at it," came from Captain Corning. "We're the finders of this, and nobody else, and it's ours by right of discovery. The ship was abandoned on the high sea, so to speak, and even Olesen and Amend had no idea where it drifted to. I think the best thing we can do is to set sail for Texas and place the stuff where the Mexicans can't get their hands on it."

"Have you any idea what this stuff is worth?" asked Andy.

"No, my lad. But it's worth a good many thousands of dollars. Why, those pearls alone would foot up to a good many thousands, and so would that diamond cross and the other jewelry."

Much of the stuff recovered was tarnished and dirty, and while the *Firefly* was on the way to Galveston the boys spent many hours in sorting out the various things and cleaning them. After this the money, jewelry, and pearls were placed in two trunks and the silver- and goldware wrapped in paper and placed in pillow cases.

"Gosh all gingersnaps!" exclaimed Randy, after this task had been finished. "I'll say we're the lucky fellows! First we capture those two bandits and then we discover this treasure!"

"It's going to mean a lot to our folks, Randy," said Jack. "If we get a fair amount from this discovery and also get the rewards for capturing Ditini and Ronombo, we'll be able to help our folks very much."

As soon as the yacht arrived at Galveston the boys and the captain had the treasure properly boxed and then shipped to New York City in care of The Rover Company. This done, the diver was paid off and the *Firefly* was placed in charge of Nat Brooks, who had orders to take the vessel back to Brooklyn. In the meanwhile the boys sent a telegram home, telling briefly of what had been accomplished.

Then another surprise awaited the youths. Less than two hours later came a reply from Tom Rover who had just gone back to New York from the mines in the West, where he had fixed up all the difficulties to his satisfaction.

Telegram received. Congratulations. Richard Rover at Old Plantation Hotel Galveston. Great News.

"Why, my dad is at the Old Plantation Hotel!" exclaimed Jack. "And Uncle Tom says there is great news! Come on, we'll go to the hotel at once!"

At the old hostelry they ran into Dick Rover as he was about to go out. Jack's father was more than astonished to see them and delighted when told of their success in locating the *Margarita*.

"I've heard already about the capture of Ditini and Ronombo," said Dick Rover. "And we've been able to make Ronombo confess that he and Ditini got half of the loot while Brown and Martell got the other half which they were to divide between themselves, Greene, Koswell, Pelter, Japson, and several others."

"I suppose the others included Crabtree," remarked Fred.

"No, the old man was to be left out in the cold, along with another man who has also been rounded up. Those fellows are going to turn state's evidence if it becomes necessary to use them. But there is still more to tell," went on Dick Rover, with a smile.

"What's that, Dad?" asked Jack quickly.

"The detectives followed Ken Greene to Galveston after you found out where he was bound, and later they learned that the Martells and the Browns had left Buffalo for this same city. They came down here, and as soon as I heard of what was going on I left the oil fields in the upper part of the state and came down also. After some difficulty we located Greene and then found out where the whole gang were to assemble. We notified the authorities and they set a guard, and as a consequence the whole crowd are now in custody in this city. As soon as we can get the necessary extradition papers we'll have them taken to New York."

"And what of the securities?" put in Randy.

"The securities apportioned to Slogwell Brown and Nelson Martell were found in a room at their hotel and are now in my possession. We have also recovered eight thousand dollars' worth of the ten thousand dollars that Ditini had and about three-quarters of the stuff with which Black Ronombo made off. He had sold some of the bonds, and these we are now trying to trace."

It may be added here that the search for the missing securities was prosecuted with vigor, and as a result of this all of the valuables taken from the offices in Wall Street were recovered with the single exception of one one-thousand-dollar Liberty Bond. And let us also add that before the year came to a close every one of those concerned in the hold-up but Josiah Crabtree was tried for the crime and sent to prison. Crabtree, old and broken, was allowed to go his way, the Rovers giving him a small amount of money to keep him from starving.

There was some dispute regarding the rewards offered for the capture of Ditini and Ronombo, but the claim of the Rover boys was prosecuted with vigor and in the end they received forty thousand dollars, which amount they divided equally.

Experts had to be called in to inspect the treasure from the *Margarita*, and then the various articles were disposed of, some in a purely commercial way and others as art treasures. The total value of the collection footed up to one hundred and twenty thousand dollars, of which the boys received eighty thousand dollars.

"Gee, we'll be millionaires before we know it!" cried Andy, dancing around when he heard of this. "I'll be getting twenty thousand dollars out of this and ten thousand dollars for capturing those bandits. That will give me thirty thousand dollars. Why, I won't know what to do with so much money!"

"I'm going to invest my money in The Rover Company," said Jack promptly.

"And so am I," added Fred.

"Well, I guess we can do that too, even if we aren't going into the business," came from Randy, and his twin nodded assent.

In addition to the money received as a reward for the capture of the bandits and the sum received from the treasure the four lads also got back nearly nine thousand dollars of the money advanced to finance the hunt for the *Margarita*.

There was one thing that pleased Jack even more than the finding of the treasure. This was a letter he received from Ruth. In that communication the girl told how her mother had recovered from the illness caused by the hold-up and how sorry her parent was over what she had said concerning the loss. Then Ruth told of how her father, after fixing up his troubles with the contractors who were building his new home, had changed his mind and gone to Sam Rover while Dick and Tom were away on business and offered to assist the Company in every way possible. She added that her father was evidently ashamed of the attitude he had first taken and hoped that Jack would forget it.

A little later in the communication Ruth mentioned some social affairs and said that Joe Sedley had called upon her twice and had wanted her and her mother to go on an extended automobile tour with him, but that she had declined.

"On an auto tour with Sedley!" grumbled Jack. "I like that! I'll make that fellow keep off the grass!" Thereupon he wrote an eight-page letter to Ruth, telling her of the many things that had occurred and of how he now intended to settle down and go into business with his father and of some things that he hoped would happen afterwards. Then he said he was coming to see Ruth as soon as he could get away.

While Jack was writing this letter to Ruth Fred was equally busy on a communication addressed to May Powell. Andy caught the youngest Rover writing this letter and did not hesitate to poke fun at him.

"Sour grapes, Andy!" returned Fred shamelessly. "You'd fall for a girl like May in a minute if you could only find one."

"No girls in mine—at least, not yet," returned the fun-loving Rover. "I'm going to be a happy bachelor, and Randy says he's going to be the same."

It must be confessed that Jack's heart beat as it had never beat before when he took the train to call on Ruth. How would she receive him after all that had passed and after the letter he had written?

But if he had any fears, they were all groundless, for when the train arrived at the town where Ruth lived he found her waiting for him at the railroad station and when she came up she not only shook hands but showed that she expected far more, and after one searching look into her clear and steady eyes, he kissed her.

"Is it all right, Ruth?" he whispered. "Tell me, is it?"

"Why, of course it is, Jack," she said softly. "It always was."

"Then Joe Sedley—"

"Oh, Jack, please don't mention that fellow! I'd rather forget him!"

"Then we can announce our engagement?"

"Any time you want to," and thereupon Ruth led the happiest fellow in the world to the automobile she had waiting.

———◇———

And now let me add a few words more and then bring to a close this story of the Rover boys.

As he had said he would do, Jack that winter invested his money in The Rover Company and Fred did likewise. At the same time Ruth's engagement to the oldest of the Rover boys was announced, and this was followed shortly by the announcement of May Powell's engagement to Fred. Then the two girls were tendered a reception at the homes on Riverside Drive and the three houses there were thrown wide open to the Stevensons, the Powells, and the many friends and relatives of all the interested families.

"I'm going to buckle down to business first," said Jack, in answer to a question from his old chum, Gif. "Mrs. Stevenson thinks that Ruth might wait a little bit before we have the knot tied." And as Fred and May were even younger, it was decided that they should wait also.

"Well, Randy and I haven't got to wait for anybody!" said Andy gayly. "So we'll just continue to roam around and have good times."

And roam he and his brother did for many years, having all sorts of adventures in which Jack and Fred often joined.

"I'll tell you this is a pretty good old world after all," declared Jack one day, when talking over their various adventures with his cousins.

"I'll say it is!" said Fred.

"I wouldn't want it any better!" came from Randy.

"It's all to the merry!" chimed in Andy.

And here, wishing all of the Rover boys the best of luck, we will say good-bye.